Praise for

Once More, With Feeling

"Tragically funny, stark, and brisk, Sophie McCreesh's brilliant debut about a young woman on the cusp perfectly captures that liminal period between youth and adulthood, being high and coming down, making stuff and becoming a real artist. She reminds me of a modern day Jane Bowles or Jean Rhys in her pitilessly honest depiction of what drinking does to and for the soul. Entrancing from start to finish."
—Lisa Gabriele, nationally bestselling author of *The Winters*

"What a compelling debut—from the very first page, Sophie McCreesh's novel hits you with brutality, charm, terror, and guts. Every chapter made me twist with anguish and then laugh out loud, a remarkable study of the utter agony that comes with being young and self-destructive. *Once More, With Feeling* is one of those books that makes you feel a little less alone in how deeply alone you actually feel, a perfect salve for our hyper-anxious and hyper-connected age."
—Scaachi Koul, nationally bestselling author of *One Day We'll All Be Dead and None of This Will Matter*

"Sophie McCreesh has written an understated and brilliant work that explores how for young women being ambitious can be terrifying and asking for what they need shameful. Jane moves through a disaffected world making open-eyed observations, which she interprets as callous, but read as touching and empathic. Although Jane is convinced she is a sociopath, her tragedy is to care too much. A random slight at a party can send her into a spiral of despair and self-loathing. Jane is a wondrous character whose terrible life choices are both fascinating and heartbreakingly tender. Although no one around her can seem to love her, the reader most certainly does."
—Heather O'Neill, award-winning author of *The Lonely Hearts Hotel*

"Heart-breaking, funny, and poignant, *Once More, With Feeling* is a beautifully subtle, unflinching balancing act of a novel. A striking and memorable accomplishment."
—Iain Reid, award-winning author of *I'm Thinking of Ending Things* and *Foe*

Once

More,

With

Feeling

Once More, With Feeling

Sophie McCreesh

ANCHOR
CANADA

Anchor Canada and colophon are registered trademarks of
Penguin Random House Canada Limited

Library and Archives Canada Cataloguing in Publication

Title: Once more, with feeling / Sophie McCreesh.
Names: McCreesh, Sophie, author.
Identifiers: Canadiana (print) 20210154462 | Canadiana (ebook) 20210154470 |
ISBN 9780385696173 (hardcover) | ISBN 9780385696180 (EPUB)
Subjects: LCGFT: Novels.
Classification: LCC PS8625.C75 O53 2021 | DDC C813/.6—dc23

This book is a work of fiction. Names, characters, places and incidents are
products of the author's imagination or are used fictitiously. Any resemblance
to actual events or locales or persons, living or dead, is entirely coincidental.

Cover and book design: Jennifer Griffiths
Cover photo: Painted Wood/Stocksy

Printed in Canada

Published in Canada by Anchor Canada,
a division of Penguin Random House Canada Limited

www.penguinrandomhouse.ca

10 9 8 7 6 5 4 3 2 1

Penguin
Random House
ANCHOR CANADA

Once More,
With Feeling

one

The music is a record of the body. One that plays back in cycles like drops of rain that will reach the ground through all the pollution and disgrace they fall into after the clouds have let them go. Maybe a body would hit a cloud like a brick if a person ever jumped from the hatch of a plane, plunging into a cluster of shattering ice crystals. But what altitude would it have to fall from in order for the clouds to be hard? Could someone drown in a cloud if they were close enough to slip into it like it was water? It would be cold. Jane has heard that hypothermia is the best kind of death—uncomfortable, then numb, an interaction with opiate receptors—how long would it take? Fog is a cloud you can breathe in.

A question from Jane's lover: "Will you chill with this depressing music?"

"'Famous Blue Raincoat' is considered the saddest song, statistically." Jane is balancing a Bluetooth mini-speaker in the palm of her hand. Her arm is erect while she's on her back in bed. She bought it in white and is beginning to detest the look of the cheap plastic. "The saddest song ever."

She's next to someone she loves in a familiar yet desperate way, and she does not believe her admiration is reciprocated.

"Says who?" The softness of his voice evokes that of someone older, more tired. She often wonders if the relationship is a useful tool in her subconscious quest for isolation, avoiding other people and staying in with this guy. Richard is twelve years older than Jane. When Jane met him, she thought they'd fuck for a few weeks and never speak again but they've been dating for over a year. Richard writes about what he claims are lucid dreams. Jane can only remember her own when she's not drinking. It takes her about three or four days off the sauce for her to be able to remember anything that happens while she's sleeping. Except for one slow dream.

Richard told her she's a great fuck and she thanked him then stared at a wall—always a fulfilling experience for Jane as she relishes in her own stagnation, settling into the buzzing of her neurotic body. He claims he loves her.

"It's just a fact." The speaker falls off her palm. Now engulfed in an aquamarine duvet, the sound is muffled in a way that heightens the effect of the tone and lyrics. "The sad music doesn't bring me down the way you might think it does."

"Over and over you play this sadness." Richard reaches into the duvet like someone who is trying to find their keys in a deep bag. His eyes move to the ceiling with a look of skepticism possibly related to what he'll find under the covers. He grabs her ass then rests his hand underneath it.

"I appreciate music more when the song lasts over seven minutes." Jane twirls her hair and stares at the ceiling while she says this, careful and calculated because she feels that this explanation of her musical taste will finally make Richard understand her.

Richard's face looks composed. He's listening this time.

"Must be long. It's an exercise in restraint—the best songs are," Jane continues.

"I see," he says, "what else?"

"I don't know how long Leonard Cohen made this song."

"Leonard Cohen can do whatever."

"It's all about repetition and subtle variations."

"'Famous Blue Raincoat'? I thought it was about drugs." He moves his hand away, resting it under his head.

"I like to just say 'songs.'"

"What?"

"Instead of 'music.'"

"What do you mean?"

"Instead of asking someone if they want to listen to music you ask them if they'd like to listen to some songs. I want to make it a thing."

"Why?"

"Music implies a strong investment."

"In what?"

"I just mean like, music has the same amount of resonance as the word poetry, if you take those things seriously enough."

"Amount of resonance?"

"Yes."

"You sound like a robot."

"Anyone who talks about music sounds arrogant."

"But the people who make it—"

"The real winners."

"So you say songs?"

"Yes, I make myself sound silly." Jane crunches her nose and looks down, the thing she does if she is embarrassed, or pretending to look embarrassed.

"Poetry, I think, is better," Richard whispers.

"Soon we will only be able to listen to one musical note. One note for a long time."

"The subtlety. I wish you had that." Again Richard grabs at Jane like she's a fruit fly that he's trying to swat away. He laughs hard as she squirms in the covers.

"Music does the subtlety too. I don't think I can explain it to you unless you already know." Jane doesn't have the attention span for poetry unless she reads it out loud.

She pauses and adjusts her body under the duvet to be

closer to Richard and closer to his cock. "Music is a way of coping with the long game."

Richard looks down at his chest and traces the tattoo of a mermaid that he has on his stomach—one he got when he was even younger than Jane is. "At least the song is lasting as long as our conversation is." The speaker makes a punishing beeping sound and a complacent recorded voice announces that the power will run out soon.

There is a permission of silence as Richard stretches over the covers for the speaker. When his hand has located the block of plastic Jane reaches for it, but he's holding it higher than she's willing to stretch. He traces his arm in the air, pretending that he's going to throw it across the room. He laughs at her a little bit, then places it on the wooden side table that Jane found on the side of the road and painted white one day, all by herself. Now they're listening to nothing but the sounds of their bodies working and breathing.

Before their conversation about songs Jane had come a lot. Now she's tired and doesn't feel like talking anymore. She turns onto her side and wraps the covers around her face, leaving only a small hole for her to breathe through. The last thing she takes in before she falls to sleep is Richard's face as he mouths "fuck" and gets out of bed. Maybe to take care of something the cat knocked over, probably its water bowl.

—

When Jane wakes up she licks her fingers and runs them under her eyes in case there is any makeup smudged there, something she dislikes. She checks her phone and sees that it is three in the morning. Richard is awake, texting.

"I dreamt it again."

"What?"

Jane acknowledges Richard's confusion. She hasn't told him about the dream. The dream where she was staying in a castle located in a dripping countryside of equal doom and glamour, a building surrounded by fields with a forest behind them protecting everything like a slow death of mazes. She could have been in England.

This is her favourite dream because it feels more real than her life.

In the dream, Jane had settled into the car she was being driven in, or was it a horse and carriage? It could have been whatever she wanted.

It took a long time to get to the castle. The driver often lost their way.

They were driving up a winding road and the setting turned into one reminiscent of an old cartoon about vampires, with the dismal sky, the lightning, and wild bats flying around the top towers of the place.

Some time passed in a nondescript way, then she blinked and she was inside the dark castle lined with velvet banners, red. Shadows were dancing in between the light from gothic candle holders that stood on the floor. She was looking for the salt-water pool.

As she wandered around, taking in various oil portraits of women who looked like they knew something she didn't, Jane became overwhelmed with a feeling—that she was very alone and also in danger.

Every time she tried to walk down one of the high corridors the doorways and connections of the hallway would move and change, but she knew there were two sides of the building and that both had working elevators. The pool was becoming important to her dream self. She wanted to have a nice swim. In order to do that she had to get to the other side of the castle as that was the side with the pool, and these abstract facts about this collection of walls seemed like her only hope for survival.

Jane walked methodically while counting the number of steps she was taking until she reached one of the elevators. She understood then that the pool was on the fifth floor, the knowledge coming to her like the embarrassment of an obvious mistake, one that is realized only when it's too late.

Inside the elevator, the button for the fifth floor was missing. In fact, all the floors with odd numbers were omitted from the gold panel. She waved, watching a thousand little versions of her arm wave back in the reflection of the mirrored walls, and took in the dress she hadn't noticed she was wearing. A small black slip. She didn't recognize her own face.

Jane thought the elevator on the other side of the castle might grant access to the floors with odd numbers. Then she got a terrible feeling in her chest and heart. She was troubled by a new fact, that a force outside herself was preventing her from getting to the salt-water pool.

Then Jane's body flashed forward in time. She was joining a party outside the castle. There were a bunch of young people like her, watching clips from old movies projected onto a white screen that was hanging on a wall. The clips seemed to change every five seconds. She recognized some of the films they were taken from—mostly Tarkovsky and Bergman films with some scenes from Andrzej Zulawski's *Possession*. Someone was setting up some music equipment on a white plastic table in the corner. Jane wanted to talk to him. The olive-green slacks he was wearing made him look like a person of substance. He looked similar to Richard but with a more generous face, the face of someone who could build her a shed or fix a rigid door. Jane went over.

He walked away as soon as she approached the table, heading to the other side of the room where there was a large box of cables on top of a velvet armchair. Jane tried to recover from the rejection by walking in a deliberate circle. She hoped no one had noticed. The room wasn't very big. It was easy for her to lightly step to the middle of the floor where there was a large green carpet set in front of the projection screen. She sat with a couple of other people. Jane asked what they were doing. Was there somewhere to go dancing? She told them that she was staying in the castle nearby.

They said they had never heard of it. Even as she described it to them, pointing in the direction of her lodgings, they shook their heads the way people do when they are asked directions but don't know the way. It was then that Jane knew she was staying in a castle no one else could see.

"Cool dream," Richard replies, anticlimactically.

"Yeah, I have it a lot. Always looking for something in the castle."

"When we get married, it'll be in a castle."

"Married?"

"I need to marry you so people don't think I'm insane dating someone so young."

"Oh, okay." Jane turns over and is comforted by the slowing pace of her thoughts. None of the bad memories are coming to her and every little social interaction she has had during the day floats away. She's not lingering on them like she usually does. Jane welcomes sleep.

A few days later she is back with Richard. This time they have been drinking all afternoon.

"Black lingerie is so boring," he snorts. Jane is touching herself but she can't get into it because Richard keeps reading this book he brings everywhere out loud. She worked in a lingerie shop a while back and still wears the outfits she stole.

"You don't like this?"

"No, I love it," he smiles and Jane stops touching herself.

"What are you thinking about?" Richard asks. Jane wants to respond that, at twenty-three, she is too young to understand current events but thinks about killing herself often.

"I'm thinking about when I first felt sad."

"You still seeing that therapist woman?"

"She's not an *official* psychotherapist anymore."

Anna lost her practitioner's license because her husband learned of an affair between Anna and one of her clients, among other things.

"Yeah, but she cares about you. You saved her kid."

GIRL SAVES DROWNING TODDLER

Jane Berkeley, thirteen, is a local hero after saving a young child from drowning in the Holiday Inn swimming pool. "I just saw this little body running to the deep end," says Jane, a seventh-grade honour roll student at the local elementary school. "She dove in and I realized she was too young to swim." Jane dropped her ice cream cone and dove into the water after the infant.

The parents were in the hot tub. Anna Stewart, the child's mother, a prominent psychologist in the community, claims she owes Jane her child's life. There have been no inquiries into her ability to care for the child. "Jane stands as an example of bravery to young folks everywhere," says Anna, who will be presenting Jane with a medallion to signify her courage, in a ceremony attended by the community.

Her mother had insisted that she wear the medal the next school day after the quaint ceremony. Anna had been there, as well as the mayor of the small suburban town in which they all lived. Jane had felt pleased with herself mostly because her parents seemed pleased with her. This pride in their daughter was a rarity. They were happy which meant that they might not scream at each other which meant that Jane felt a sense of accomplishment. She'd been able to keep the peace. They shouted often.

Jane's mother thought that the medal would help Jane fit in. It could serve as a conversation piece. Jane believed her, wearing the bronzed medal over her blue Gap sweater to school the next day. A perfectly reasonable thing for a thirteen-year-old to do.

No one paid much attention to Jane or her accessories. It was beginning to disturb her. Near the end of class, she decided to make an announcement. She raised her hand.

"Yes, Jane?" Mrs. Hallows placed both her hands neatly in front of her while she waited for Jane to respond.

"I have a medal."

"Yes, I see you do. I read about this in the paper. Everyone, let's give Jane a round of applause."

"Why are we giving her a round of applause?" The kids in her class had been together for about eight years by now, as they were the only ones in the French immersion program. The boy who was asking was one of the more popular kids. His name was Henry and he was known for his Pokémon card collection and for being good at football.

Jane felt stupid all of a sudden. She whispered, "Because I saved someone who was drowning."

"Way to brag!" Henry yelled. This was followed by some laughter from the other kids until Mrs. Hallows raised her voice.

"Hush now. Jane has done a good thing." She added tenderly, "Congratulations."

The bell rang for lunch. Jane ran to catch up with some of the girls she usually ate with. They never waited for her to get her stuff from her locker so she had collected everything already. They were all standing around Henry.

When Jane joined the circle, no one acknowledged her. They were talking about Myspace. One of the other girls was promising Henry that she would put him in her Top Friends. Henry smiled and said, "You better." Then he turned to Jane. "Can I wear your medal?"

"No."

"Wow, can't even part with her precious medal." Everyone picked up on the "wow," joining in like a chorus. They laughed.

Jane took the medal off and handed it to Henry. He put it on and then ran away to join some other guys who were carrying skateboards.

Over the next month, Anna would invite Jane and her parents over for dinner parties at the house she shared with her then-husband, one with three garage doors. She'd always cook the same thing, penne with pesto. Years later, Jane would realize that this was the only thing Anna knew how to make or had the energy to.

Once Jane's parents realized that Anna was a therapist, they secured her services for free because Jane was acting out and they didn't want to pay for a real one. The wait for a therapist provided by the government would be too long. Her mother had been suspicious since finding an empty metal container full of ashes under Jane's bed. She'd stuck her fingers in the ash searching for cigarette butts only to find remnants of photographs taken of Jane as a child.

Jane had overheard her mother's phone conversation with Anna while listening from the vent in her room. She knew that although Anna was a registered psychotherapist, she wasn't technically allowed to treat Jane because they already knew each other.

"You can consider it a simple conversation, not an actual session." Jane heard her mother's voice change to a heightened tone that was unusual for her to use on the phone. Desperation.

They began to hold sessions in Anna's living room during the evenings. Jane didn't mind. She liked going to Anna's house because it was nicer than hers and the red leather La-Z-Boy chairs that she had comforted her. Anna had bought a package of assorted tea biscuits that she placed carefully on a silver dish on the table in between them. She poured two cups of chamomile tea. She sat down and stared patiently at Jane, as if she had all the time in the world to wait. Jane was silent.

"Your mother says you've been destroying photographs of yourself."

They continued to sit in silence for a few minutes until Anna asked, "Who's your favourite parent?"

"My dad."

"Who is your best friend at school?"

"I get angry at the others. They make fun of me."

"Are you sure?"

"I feel like something really bad is going to happen," Jane admitted.

"Like what?"

"My chest hurts all the time."

"Jane, you are in a safe place. What if we try a different approach?"

"Okay." Jane felt timid and impatient, like she had some place to be that wasn't Anna's living room.

"If you had a magic wand, what would you change?" Anna paused between each word, making the question sound condescending.

"I'd be less lonely. Prettier."

"There is nothing physically wrong with you."

"Have you seen me?"

Jane began to wonder if she was being filmed. She felt as if she were in some test situation where she'd been asked to draw something or write a poem, and her potential for innovation and intelligence would be judged by the specificity of her creation.

"Jane, you are a very bright girl."

"How do you know that?"

"I can tell. It's in your eyes."

"You just met me."

"You have already shown such ingenuity."

"What does *ingenuity* mean?"

"It means that you're clever and resourceful."

"Anna," Jane said in a forced tone that she thought would capture her therapist's attention, or at least project confidence, "I want to make nice art at some point."

"Are you good at making art?"

"I don't think so. But I will do whatever it takes to be good. I will put in the time."

"Jane, what kind of artist do you want to be?"

"I don't know yet."

"Why art?"

"It's easier to be alone that way."

"Why do you want to be alone?"

"I don't know if I want to be. It's just easier to see feelings than to feel them all by yourself."

Jane's bed is beginning to smell like an old sock. Not that she notices. The covers are sticky mostly because Richard sweats a lot at night. She's just happy to be there, eager and willing. Richard puts his arm around Jane and props himself up with a large pillow. Jane keeps her head down on the bed, resulting in her hair being nestled in Richard's armpit.

"Is she the one who always comments on your photos?" Richard asks when Anna's photo flickers across the screen.

"Yeah, she's pretty much the only one who does."

"She's kind of weird."

"She's just older."

"No, it's something more."

"What?"

"I looked at her profile once and it just seems like she acts younger than she is. I know it's bad to say that people should act their age, but while I went through her photos, I had this feeling that I wanted to look away, but couldn't."

"Let's talk about something else."

"It makes me sad. She seems, like, desperate. She's hot, though."

"Can you please fuck off."

"She acts like she's your age with her selfies and everything. Desperate, like you."

"I'm not desperate." Jane's response is a touch defensive, too quick.

"You are, a little."

"Stop it."

"Don't know why you're desperate. I'm right here." Richard puts both his arms in the air and begins to wiggle his body around as if he's dancing.

"I feel old." Jane's really just too hungover to think properly. She feels like an idiot.

"How?"

"I look at my face in the mirror and it seems like it belongs to an older person. Someone who has seen a lot and is just tired. I experience no wisdom."

"Do I look old?" Richard twists his body so that his face is directly in front of Jane's. He makes a kissy face.

"You look angry all the time unless you're fucking, or listening to techno. You could moisturize your skin more."

Richard pauses as if to process what Jane has just said. Then he does something that surprises them both. He laughs, hard.

Jane has to control herself because it's better if she doesn't laugh with him. "But seriously, have I put too much bad shit into my body?"

"Jane." Richard is himself again, with his mean face and smiling eyes. He places two fingers in front of his eyes then hers. The gesture strikes her as unexpected and false. It turns her off. She's listening, though. "I have put extraordinary things in my body. I have degraded myself in ways I hope you never understand. But look how charming I am now."

Everything has become quite serious.

"In high school, I used to eat paper instead of food. Every other hour I would let myself have a cracker with honey on it."

"I think you need to try acid."

"I probably should."

two

When Jane was a lot younger, there was a man who would sit on his roof and spray all of the neighbourhood kids with a high-powered water gun. Everyone loved it. One time Jane saw him in the front seat of his car, bent over, pouring a bottle of beer into a steel water bottle.

She walked up to him and said, "What's that?"

He stopped pouring and leered at Jane with the hint of a smile. His car—a jeep—gave him more height than usual over her. "Only for adults." He resumed pouring. He shut the door of the jeep.

Jane ran through the three grassy yards that separated the strange man's house from hers. She would tell her parents what she had just seen. She knew that the man was drinking the same stuff that made her mom sad and her dad frustrated with his surroundings.

If she closed her eyes, she'd still know that she had reached her own yard by the feeling of brittle grass breaking in between her toes, through her sandals. There was a dying birch tree in the middle of the front lawn. One time she'd climbed on it and her neighbour, a boy her age who called her gross and ugly, shook the tree until she fell out.

She stopped on her front porch to rub the dirt off her legs and feet, checking her reflection in the window beside the door in case there was dirt on her face, too. She turned the knob of the front door and then tried the doorbell, peering through the window when she found the door locked.

Like most of the houses in the suburbs, hers had two garage doors that held contents protected by a keypad with a special code. Jane could have walked around to the side door of the garage to let herself in. But she sat on the porch and waited, not because she wanted someone to answer the door, but because she wanted someone to come up to her and ask the right questions. She wanted to think straight.

Richard arrives at Jane's door with a pizza and some groceries for Jane, including a box of tampons because Jane refuses to buy them on principle. He's tall enough that Jane has to lift her head up to look at him. She doesn't know why she lets him buy things for her. It makes her feel sick, in the sense that she should feel guilty but doesn't. The thought of doing something vaguely productive for her art allows her mind to float away from purgatory.

She phones Anna often, while Richard snores beside her, and Anna tells her not to trust her thoughts. To do the opposite. Anna claims that Jane has mind-fucked herself into a psychological trap of non-being due to her depression and inherent anxiety. Not to mention acute paranoia. She suggests Jane join a yoga class.

"Check out this livestream of *Abbey Road*." Richard has moved into bed with his pizza and Jane is terrified he's going to drop it on the covers. That she'll have to pay for the laundromat sooner than expected. He's fixated on the screen of his phone.

"Why would I ever want to do that?"

"Fuck off. It's interesting." He laughs as he finishes the crust of the pizza, which is stuffed with delicious plastic cheese. Richard licks his fingers. Beautiful, with a tan that stays all year, along with sombre green eyes that make him appear to be listening intently even when he's not. He is skinny like the heroin-chic ads from the nineties. He has toned arms and abs that don't go away even when he eats pizza in bed. He claims his arms are toned because he is a strong lumberjack who chops wood with one hand and writes poetry with the other.

"Why not watch something more interesting, like videos of kinetic sculptures?" She feels dependent on him for emotional support these days, because she has lost the ability to feel happy. She wonders if she ever carried such a skill.

Jane has this theory of the well-adjusted person. Someone who is many things: they wear a sports bra to support their small breasts while they do yoga, they have over one thousand followers on Instagram, they pose for photographs on top of mountains, they post videos of themselves singing while making homemade bread, a bottle of beer can last them an hour. They take selfies whenever they enter a new phase of their life and write long captions explaining whatever lesson they have learned, what you too should learn. They've put a lot of thought into their personal brand. They are sent shoes, clothes, and makeup by shops that they tag on their Instagram accounts. They have more than two friends that they've known since kindergarten. They are calm and pleasant to talk to. Nothing bad has ever happened to the well-adjusted so they assume the world will always be ready to receive them in all their positivity and grace.

Jane would do anything to become a well-adjusted person. She studies them like they're animals in a nature documentary because they are foreign to her.

She remembers Anna lecturing her about deriving happiness from specific end-goals and how this can be detrimental, meaning that she shouldn't base her happiness on external forces: *I'll be happy if I achieve such and such. I'll be happy if Richard supports me emotionally. I will be happy if I get to travel.* Jane assumes that her emotions will level out once she starts school. Then her feelings of uselessness will go away. But she feels reluctant to place such value on her own productivity, not just because she hates the concept of productivity in itself.

She often takes personality tests online. Myers-Briggs, astrology, attachment styles, emotional skills and competence, as well as that one that tells her she is a director and a negotiator. She does them drunk and then she'll do them again sober, messaging Richard and asking him to remind her of the day he was born so she can check their compatibility. Asking him about his Myers-Briggs results—whether or not his four letters start with an "I" or an "E." The tests are both hilarious and unnerving to her as she picks out traits she likes and repeats harsh internal dialogue about the ones she doesn't. *I would have acted differently if I'd known I was an INT—?* To what extent do folks act differently when they have been told how they are? That they're sensitive and deeply intuitive as a Pisces, or that they want to stay home and drink because they are an introvert and going out would be too much without a little something. Talking to other humans is just too much. She doesn't really believe in it.

Jane walks home along Bloor Street, peering into cars drudging through the morning traffic until the drivers notice her.

A woman wearing a black skirt with white paint on it is standing next to a candy store. She holds a bag of British Hula Hoops in one hand, a cigarette in the other, and seems transfixed by the stuffed Homer Simpson toy in the window. She doesn't move for two minutes. Jane has stopped as well, to smoke. From across the street, Jane stands and watches. She wants to teach the woman about happiness so she won't be stuck in purgatory like Jane is. In order to do that, Jane will have to learn how to process life's little humiliations. She pulls out her phone to call Anna but ends up looking in the camera again, obsessing over each line that's formed under her eyes. She is dialling Anna's number when Scotty, Richard's best friend, appears and interrupts her.

"Come to this show tonight." He holds his cigarette like it's a joint.

"Maybe. If I get off work early." Jane is lying. She isn't scheduled to work.

"There's free beer. Bring Richard."

"Do I have your number?"

"Put yours in my phone." Scotty lunges his hand into a purple backpack with square green pockets and pulls out what appears to be a brand-new phone, along with a small plastic box. Scotty always has the latest gadgets. He is about Jane's height, which is shorter than average for a woman. He's thick-boned with red hair and freckles that vary in size and shape, the bigger ones across his nose. While Jane enters her number into his new phone, she notes the time. Close to ten. Then Scotty shows her what he claims is a portable 3D printer, waving the small plastic box in her face then putting it deep in his pocket as if he has to hide it, from everyone. Jane needs friends other than Richard and Scotty.

"Well." She hands back the phone. "I'm off. I need to get . . ."

Scotty indicates a detour she can take in order to pass the liquor store—and that's not something you can state outright to someone. It's more of a nod-glance type thing. Maybe Scotty is all right after all. Scotty knows what Jane likes.

Next to the liquor store, there's a handsome man who's giving out free popcorn to get people to sign up for a smartphone app. He hands her an iPad and Jane enters the made-up e-mail she gives to companies she never wants to hear from again. All this lying just for free popcorn, just to talk to someone hot. The man's name tag reads *Chase*. Jane doesn't like the name Chase, but she's certain she can get around it. But Chase doesn't notice her as he stares at his equally attractive co-worker, who is dressed in another version of his red uniform. The woman is wearing a tight, short, red sport-dress. Jane informs the handsome man that she plans to break up with her boyfriend. He gives her double the amount of popcorn and greets another set of pedestrians.

The truth is as follows:

She'd been fucking Richard since five this morning.

She's just noticed a zit inside her earlobe.

It will take a minimum of two weeks for the zit to be ready to pop.

The popcorn tastes like aspartame and vomit.

Jane sighs as she enters the liquor store and turns the music in her headphones up loud. She needs to decide what to do about Richard. She feels like she's dating a loser with poor-quality friends—a reflection of how she feels about herself.

The art show turns out to be a showcase of ceramic swans with cotton swabs of the artist's DNA stuck onto them with what Jane suspects is a glue gun. Richard doesn't join her, claiming he'd prefer to drink hard liquor in bed and watch his stories. There is a disco ball in the middle of the concrete warehouse. Jane sends Richard a picture of two golden ceramic swans kissing. Then she writes: *Fuck me?*

While she leans against the wall, sipping a free craft beer with a picture of a cottage on the can, a fly buzzes onto her arm. Her nerves are shot. She jolts, knocking one of the ceramic swans onto the floor. A few people around her gasp. Scotty, who is standing nearby, walks away from her when she looks to him with pleading eyes. Jane is perpetually clumsy. It has always been this way, going back to elementary school.

She remembers her hands shaking when Mrs. Hallows handed her a small, square package with a purple condom inside. It reminded her of a gooey freeze-pop. The grade seven classes had been gathered for a sexual education seminar. Some of them had already done it, others pretended. Jane didn't care about sex. She daydreamed often about fairies. There were inspirational posters on the classroom's concrete brick walls, which were painted white. One of the posters said: *Go for it!*

"Put the condom on the wood, so you'll know how to do it in real life," Mrs. Hallows said to Jane as she pointed to a desk positioned in front of the class.

The wooden practice shaft looked like Pinocchio's nose. Jane stared at the faded posters, then the wall where their poetry was displayed. Jane's poem about woodland fairies had come in second to Beth Herrington's sonnet about dolphins.

She placed the condom on top of the shaft and pulled the sides down, but it was on the wrong way and the weird plastic wouldn't unroll properly. She used two hands to stretch it over the fake penis. This excruciating process lasted about sixty seconds but felt like an eternity to Jane. She was relieved when the condom broke. The teacher sighed and looked at her watch. "Who's next?" she called out, while the children snickered at Jane's failure.

The gasping art people go back to their business and it's as if no one noticed that the swan fell off the wall. She'll miss

Scotty, who she assumes has walked away forever. She probably would have done the same if he'd been the one to knock the swan. The cotton swab has rolled under the table where a DJ is playing. Have they been playing music the whole time? Jane doesn't understand how the artist's DNA is really on the swab and she wonders if that just means that they spat on it. Surprised that the ceramic swan didn't break when it fell, Jane moves away as well, immediately navigating a series of calming thought patterns that will allow her to forget that she has done anything embarrassing, ever. Now she's trying to place the music that's playing, or figure out who's playing, or figure out why they're playing. She hates not knowing what a track is called. There are a lot of good-looking people in the gallery. Jane wonders if she is one of them.

Jane wakes up to Richard crawling across the floor to the bathroom so he can throw up and Jane thinks *this is what love must be like* because she lets him back into her bed. It's morning. There are birds outside making their beautiful noises. He pulls out his phone.

"But what are you looking for, in the livestream?" she asks, her face on his chest as he refreshes the screen. Jane didn't think his obsession with the livestream would come up again.

"I want to see a bunch of losers re-enacting the *Abbey Road* cover."

"Aren't you more of a loser for watching?"

"Life is long, and this is what I consider fun."

"Did you tell your ex to get your name tattooed on her foot?"

"She just sent me a picture of it. I didn't know she was going to."

Jane shrugs and pulls her legs out of bed so she can go to the toilet. When Jane releases fluid into the bowl she forgets whether dark yellow is good or bad. She smells her feet. The only shoes she wants to wear to work are cheap flats from a store for teenagers with a sign on the front that's pink. They make her feet stink all the time. Last night, someone on the streetcar was covering their mouth and Jane leaned over, stuck out her foot, and asked, "Can you smell that?"

Richard has a friend other than Jane or Scotty: a mustard feline with the tenacity of a spoiled child. The cat is staying with Jane, for a while, because Richard is moving. Jane likes the fact that the cat is at her house because it means that Richard will come over more often. Richard often accuses her of not loving the cat enough, or vice versa.

"Vronsky doesn't like you."

"What are you talking about? We spent all yesterday bonding." Jane has picked up her computer on the way back from peeing. She wants to watch an ocean documentary. Richard gets up and starts moving things noisily around Jane's apartment, as if he wants attention.

"Aren't you hungover?"

"Puking helped," he says while pushing one of Jane's bookcases without bothering to take the books out. He manages to get it moving by wiggling it back and forth.

Jane wonders who she could reach out to because she's sick of dealing with the oscillating spectrum of Richard's moods. It's mostly about finding someone who isn't sick of hearing about her boyfriend. Pretty much everyone she knows has told her to drop him.

When Richard is done moving the bookcase, he seems tired again.

"The most famous psychopaths are obsessed with cats. I am one of them," he says.

"Why did you move my bookcase a metre to the left?"

"To give Vronsky more space."

"He already had space."

"Like I said, psychopaths and cats go together like milk and tears."

Jane isn't familiar with the expression, and she is suspicious he made it up. She chooses not to say anything about that.

"Who are the psychopaths?"

"I can't remember." Richard jumps back in the bed. "What are we watching?"

"An ocean documentary. Richard, you know I love your cat, as much as I love you."

"He doesn't like you."

"Why not?"

"You don't show him enough affection."

"Oh! But I do."

"I can tell you make him unhappy."

Richard is trying to provoke her. She refuses to engage.

Jane pulls her finger over the touch pad of the computer, skimming the little line under the video so that she can find the part about the bioluminescent deep-sea creatures. They watch in silence until Richard announces that he's going to see Scotty. He dresses quickly, pulling on two different-coloured socks, one blue, one grey. Jane watches Vronsky follow him to the door. "Be nice to her while I'm gone," Richard says to the cat.

Jane goes to bed alone and starts touching herself while thinking about Vronsky, of all things. Not in a weird way, but in the way that people sometimes think about what they're going to make for dinner while they're fucking. She's more than hospitable to him. She's stroked his belly. Fed him treats while looking for approval, as if the cat's approval is equivalent to Richard's, which would be equivalent to happiness.

Vronsky is a spoiled brat.

It still feels strange that she's thinking about this unrequited love as she touches the left side of her clit but she usually thinks of everyday things when she does this, never picturing anyone in particular. Maybe she's really thinking about Richard's, well, love. What it would be like to have that.

She gets up and checks who has liked the picture she posted of Vronsky the Cat. No one. She goes to the fridge and pours the rest of a cheap box of wine into a mason jar, bringing it into bed. She feels like shutting her thoughts off.

Text to Anna: *The cat does not love me. Richard does not appreciate me. I need new friends.*

She can hear the tap from her bathroom dripping at a pace that is accelerating rapidly but she can't physically move to stop it. The wine has made her feel lethargic and anxious at the same time. She tries to ignore the tap and waits for the insights of her fake therapist to pop up on her phone and guide her through another day alone.

A message from Anna: *The cat will only love you once you love yourself. Ask a friend from work for coffee. Go shopping. A sober activity.*

Jane replies that she is wildly unpopular. The cat can sense that.

At lunch Jane's parents settle themselves into the booth near the window. Her mother removes her sunglasses and puts them into a case detailed with flowers that match the yellow sundress she is wearing. Her father places his sunglasses on the table next to his phone, which he will check periodically throughout the meal.

"Why didn't the restaurant have the name on the front?" her mother asks in all earnestness.

"It's an annoying Toronto thing. None of them do." Jane fills her parents' glasses with water from the long green bottle that was placed on the table when they came in. Then she opens her menu and starts to skim for something that is both filling and expensive since she won't be paying. The problem is that she's not hungry. She doesn't see an appetite coming in the near future. She could maybe get some iron from a piece of steak if she can stomach it.

"I just don't understand how we were supposed to find the restaurant. We would have been completely lost if you didn't know it was here."

Jane turns to her father, whose eyes are taking in the colourful wallpaper around them. Most of the decor is either pink or green.

"Do you like it here, Dad?"

"Of course, it's lovely." He smiles and pats Jane's hand from across the table.

"How was your drive up?" Jane asks.

"It was quite fast. No traffic on Sundays," her mother says.

There is a silence for a beat until a server comes to their table and introduces himself as Chad.

"Hello, Chad!" Jane's father smiles. This enthusiasm is a quality that Jane likes about him. He is often jolly and silly.

"What can I get you?" Chad smiles in an exaggerated way and Jane can't tell if he is put off by her father's keenness or encouraged by it.

"I'll have a mimosa, whenever you have time." Jane adds "whenever you have time" because she too is a server and wants to make the jobs of other servers as easy as possible. She's also left wondering if it came across as passive-aggressive.

"Two glasses of the Pinot Grigio for us, please," Jane's father says. He turns to her mother. "Is that all right, darling?"

"And a bottle of sparkling water," her mother says as she folds the drink menu and places it to the side of the booth they are sitting in, leaning it against the wall as if to present it to the table.

Jane is excited for her mimosa to arrive. It might wake her up enough to be able to stomach food. She tries to think of something impressive to tell her parents so that they will think she is doing well. Not much comes to mind. All she does is work, drink, and see Richard.

"I'm excited to start school soon."

"Try not to arrive hungover on the first day," her father jokes in a way that she knows is really serious.

"You must be thrilled," her mother adds as she refills her own water glass, leaving Jane's and her dad's glasses empty.

"The Fish Bar won't be open all year." Jane works at a restaurant called the Fish Bar beside the lake. She doesn't like to tell anyone where she works.

The server returns with their drinks, placing Jane's mimosa in front of her mother. When he leaves they switch drinks.

"Why?" her mother asks.

"They only stay open when the weather permits." Jane shrugs.

"Do we know what we are ordering?" Jane's father is looking at her mother when he asks this.

"Is it okay if I get a steak?" Jane asks.

"Of course," her father says. He picks up his phone and starts to sing a song about paying the parking meter, which he is doing through an app. Jane smiles a little bit. Her mother is frowning at him and he stops singing the song when he notices.

"Very good. We're worried you're not eating properly."

"Is it true that steak speeds up your metabolism if it's undercooked, like raw?" Jane asks.

"I'm really not sure, darling, that could be just a myth." Her mother's voice is gentle.

Her father puts the phone down. "Are you going to get another job while you're in school?"

"I can try and find another bar job. It's difficult to get part-time hours at a new place, though."

Jane's mother motions to her father to move so she can get out of the booth. Jane points in the direction of the restroom and smiles. Her father sits back down, sliding over so that he is facing Jane.

"Do you have any money saved?"

"I have enough for the next bit." Jane's rent is manageable, compared to that of other people she knows. She's saved quite a bit in anticipation for the school year. To be a student who doesn't work in restaurants anymore.

The server returns and asks if they are ready. Jane's father points at her mother's empty chair. "We're waiting for the boss." He smiles. Jane thinks this is a stupid joke.

He turns his attention back to Jane. "Well, we won't let you starve. Are there grants you can apply for?"

"Yes."

"What shall we have?" He opens the menu and starts reading every item out loud. "You said you're having the steak. Perhaps I'll have that as well."

Her mother appears at the table. "Can you move, please?" she says to her father.

The server returns and Jane's mother tells him that she needs more time.

"I think I'll have a pasta," her mother announces as soon as the server leaves. The restaurant is getting busier now, or they have turned up the music which in turn makes the whole atmosphere seem chaotic. There is a short silence at the table. Her father starts dancing in his seat to the pop song that is playing.

"The weather is so warm." Her mother smiles as she turns towards the large window, into the sky.

"It usually stays warm well into September."

"Then why doesn't the Fish Bar stay open?" her dad asks.

"Maybe they will," Jane replies, even though she is hoping her time there is done, forever. That her time as a server is done. She doesn't like doing things for other people. In fact, she hates talking to anyone at all. Now it's Jane's turn to get up and go to the bathroom, mostly because she is anxious and wants to see if she can sneak outside to have a cigarette. She's grabbed a smoke and a small lighter, holding them in her hand while she smiles at both her parents. It will be an adventure, trying to get outside without them noticing. Her parents hate smoking. She doesn't want to smoke in front of them, especially since they have just offered her money.

"Order me a rare steak if he comes back. Thank you."

Like most people she knows, Jane hates being at work. She is a terrible server. When she arrives, she summons the cheap jokes needed to make her co-workers feel like they are loved, and they reply with the necessary compliments on each other's appearance. Surface acting. The energy it takes to do this drains Jane. But when something's on Jane's mind, she has to tell everyone around her. It's her weakness. Soon, the entire staff knows that her boyfriend is obsessed with his cat and the *Abbey Road* livestream.

Everyone at the Fish Bar, including Jane's kind-of-friend Kitty, thinks Richard shows signs of an unstable character.

"Richard used to be hot but now . . ." Kitty shakes her head.

"You know him?"

"Everyone does."

In high school, many people whispered about Kitty but feared her wrath at the same time. Even after leaving school, Jane continued to hear stories about her. Jane remembers one Monday alone when rumours flew that Kitty lost her virginity at a party in a barn, was dating a college guy who was a DJ, and had given three guys head at the same party. Jane used to visit Kitty's Myspace page because Kitty used it as a platform to correct rumours. *I was on my period. I couldn't possibly have slept with anyone. You're all filthy liars*, Kitty wrote in the "About Me" section of her Myspace. *DJ Todd Waits and I are just good friends.* People loved her despite the vicious rumours regarding her sexual activity. Jane thought the rumours were creepy and unfair. Kitty's denial was both brave and alluring.

One of the few times the two girls spoke in high school was in the ninth grade, when Kitty and her group of vapid girls (as Jane had named them) approached her in the cafeteria and asked if Jane had ever tried a drink. Jane had tried plenty of beer at her parents' suggestion. But she felt uncomfortable, almost choking on a chicken finger while she attempted to roll her eyes and think of labels of her parents' bottles, which were located in the same cupboard as the measuring cups she used to bake vanilla cupcakes. "Sambuca," she replied. That didn't fly, and the girls walked away laughing. Embarrassed, Jane wanted to try more alcohol immediately. She would start alone in her room, and she would later think back to this time, imagining a ghost of herself visiting with a warning.

It took Kitty a month of their working together at the restaurant to recognize Jane from high school. She'd clued in while they shared post-shift drinks late one night.

"Oh." Kitty drew out the O sound and widened her eyes as if she'd just solved a great mystery. "You're Crying Girl!"

"What?"

"People used to say you always looked like you were going to cry. Fuck. No offence. I should have recognized you."

"Do I look like that?"

"Sort of, but it's hot now."

Despite Kitty's failure to remember their rich history, she is Jane's favourite person to work with because when it's busy, she makes direct eye contact and says, "Fuck. Me." Kitty often jokes that Jane is a terrible waitress and Jane replies that it's true. Jane is an introvert. Introverts can be quite aggressive.

"I'm going back to school in the fall."

"Me too, thank god," Kitty scoffs as she walks away to take an order.

The entire restaurant is a patio apart from the "staff shack" where they sneak french fries into their mouths and chug coconut water because of the heat. At work Jane is usually hungover so she takes different vitamins that she thinks target parts of the nervous system. She has no science to back this up. Blood, calm, and energy is the combination she hopes for from the pills she orders every month: collagen, B12, vitamin C, liquid silver, probiotics, and much more.

"Did he really say that?" Jane can tell by her tone that Kitty thinks her relationship with Richard is a joke.

"Say what?" Richard says a lot of ridiculous things.

"About the cat not liking you. Verona?"

"The cat's name is Vronsky. Anyway, I'm more concerned about my work."

"What work?"

"I paint. I'm going to do an MFA."

"But are you in an abusive relationship?" Kitty's eyes are wide.

"Maybe." Jane drops a plate of nachos. "I think we might be in the same fine arts program. I saw you post about it on your Instagram."

"Congrats! Now stop dropping shit or you'll be fired."

Jane welcomes the thought of being laid off even though it means that she would have to subsidize her drug habit some other way.

———

After her shift, Jane takes a taxi home. Her work pays for them after two in the morning—any time after the subway stops running. Inside, she takes out the mickey she bought before her shift and drinks it to soothe herself enough to fall asleep. She doesn't care if the driver notices.

Something that has always bothered Jane about her apartment is the lilac paint on the white ceiling. She'd tried to paint the place without using tape that keeps the paint from getting on the wrong spot. Tonight, it's the first thing she notices when she lets herself in. Kicking off her shoes, she can make out the trace of Richard's body in her bed, asleep. Jane wonders why she ever gave him a key. She doesn't feel excited to see him, wanting solitude after speaking to strangers all day. She makes noises moving around the apartment to wake him up. Maybe he will get annoyed and leave. When he continues to sleep, she puts music on and starts dancing. She knows she's really sexy, though someone looking in would see a woman wobbling with a whiskey bottle in her hand, with old bags that once held pizza slices lying around the room. The plastic wrappers of the toothbrushes Richard keeps buying because they break up almost every day and Jane throws the old ones out.

"Can I read the book to you?" she yells into Richard's ear.

He rolls over. "You don't like doing that."

She pulls her hands through his thin hair and thinks that it might be gone in the next ten years. He's already covering up the side patches. "I thought you said you'd stop eating pizza in bed."

"Are you on the Jamie?" He means Jameson.

"No." She starts to climb on top of him.

"I'm not a jungle gym."

"You are."

"Read it to me."

Jane opens Richard's copy of J. G. Ballard's *Crash* to see that the words are moving. She reads the same line over twice and then cries out, "It's us!"

"We wish it was us."

"Can you get me a glass of water?" Jane says, motioning with her left hand towards the general direction of the fridge. She's certain there is a bottle of sparkling water there.

"It's better when I read," he says without getting up.

"Yeah, you do voices for all of them."

"Most of them sound the same."

"Dead and bored."

While Richard reads, Jane recalls that her father used to read out loud and she wonders if the fact that Richard is doing it as well has any significance. She decides that they are having a nice time and that she doesn't need to think about it. It's fine. She pays special attention to her body, making sure that she appears calm and receptive even though it's quite difficult for her to concentrate on what he is reading. A narrative is usually easy to follow. Reading a story is easier than reading a poem. She looks up at Richard who is smiling while the words come out of his mouth, like he can keep going for a long time. But Jane is wrong, he shuts the book abruptly.

"That's the end of the chapter," he declares while getting up. He walks like a cat, with languid ownership of whatever space he finds himself in. Jane likes to watch him, and it is during these moments that she wishes he would stay. He closes the door of the bathroom in the way that Jane instructed him to—turning the knob before pushing the door closed—so that it doesn't make a slamming noise.

"But not the end of our love," Jane yells as loud as she can, feigning a voice of desperate hope, so he can hear her over the fan in the bathroom. He doesn't respond.

She positions herself in what she feels is a docile sleeping position. She closes her eyes, pretending that she has entered a rejuvenating slumber without a care in the world. She hears him walk into the kitchen. Jane commits to pretending to sleep until Richard starts poking her arm with the bottle of sparkling water that she asked for earlier—not even thinking to pour it into a glass. She sits up. Only when the water reaches her lips does she realize how thirsty she is, and she begins to suck back the contents of the bottle with such force that all the air comes out of it. The bottle starts to implode, and now it's crushed in her hand.

"It looks like you're sucking a cock when you do that." Richard climbs over her and turns his back to her.

"You love it."

"I do."

"Will you tie me up again?"

Richard turns to Jane and smiles without looking at her, as if there is a friend of his nearby that he's just told a joke to. "You got scared last time."

"No I didn't." Richard had given her a talk about trust and sex and how those two things together would translate into a gorgeous expression of joy. He'd instructed her to lie down on her stomach on the bed and then he spent a long time tying her hands and ankles to the corresponding bedposts while explaining what kind of knots he was using. When it was all done Jane lay there thinking about how it was now impossible to reach her drink. She wondered if she would be okay. If Richard might hurt her. She felt frightened in her body like she was out of control. Maybe that was the point. Maybe someone had already hurt her and she didn't remember. She pulled at her wrists in the ropes to see if she could break free if she wanted to, then she waited a few moments before she said, "Untie me, I'm scared"—but it all came out as one word.

"That won't happen again," she said.

"We could just do chair time?" Chair time is what they call Richard tying Jane to a chair and fucking her.

"Chair time is nice." She doesn't know how the chair is any different from the bed.

"You love chair time." He nestles his head into his pillow.

"Maybe later," she says.

Some time passes and Richard has fallen asleep. The details of his eyes look like they've been painted on when closed because the lashes vary in length, reminding Jane of the branches of a willow tree. Jane is on her back, awake for a long time thinking about what it would be like to date someone different. Richard is mean, but not cruel. If she were a well-adjusted person, she would cut off all contact with this man and find a new one. He'd be slightly worse-looking than Jane, but he'd be so nice.

three

"Do you come with the entrée?" asks the man at the table she's serving, after Jane has explained the oyster specials. It's easy to drink at the Fish Bar, and Jane no longer feels guilty about it because she has to deal with such vile, unreasonable people. Besides, summer is almost over and this place rarely hires people back on, not that she'd want it. Her fine arts program begins in the coming weeks and things might be better then.

"No," Jane responds, feeling a mixture of repulsion towards the man and pity for herself for her timid response.

"We'll have four east coast oysters and eight west coast oysters. Did you get that?" The man looks to his friends as if he expects them to laugh while adjusting his ill-fitting grey suit that hangs loosely in the wrong places, reminding Jane of a deflated tent.

"No, I'm not that bright." A bit better.

Jane turns and heads over to the staff shack with the POS system, where the servers keep their belongings. She feels inside her bag for her flask, deliberately forgetting to punch in the man's order for a long time. After taking a swig of her purse whiskey, she's feeling confident in her abilities as a human being. Her plan is to take Anna's advice and ask a co-worker to hang out in order to form a connection with a person who is not Richard. She has Kitty's number by the end of the night.

Kitty and Jane are already able to laugh together with their eyes. They went to the same high school and rarely spoke. They both moved here from the suburbs. It isn't an unusual story but the fact that they both come from the same place could be the foundation of some bond. Jane could be wrong. She hardly knows the girl.

It feels almost eerie to be meeting this person outside of work. Jane wonders if they'll run out of stuff to talk about. There was this other time in high school when Jane was in the change room with Kitty and her friends. They were huddled in the opposite corner whispering in sharp bursts about a party. Jane was half-listening. They were all changing after a game of indoor soccer. Jane had scored a couple of goals. The room was a large square with a bench around the edges with cubbies, as well as hooks for their everyday uniforms. In the corner there was a short hallway that led to showers and a washroom. That was where Jane was planning to go before she was cornered. This wasn't some public humiliation thing—only a handful of people were around and the whole situation was bizarre, to be honest. Still, it registered in her brain as something she needed to get revenge for.

Jane was changing her shirt and she turned around to see Kitty crawling on all fours, wearing one of those masks that people get for a masquerade ball or something—with feathers and jewels that cover half of their face. Kitty was crawling in a restrained and dramatic way towards Jane. She was purring like a feline, even stopping to lick her hand occasionally. The others were watching Kitty, alternating between "oh my god" and covering their laughing mouths. Jane had no idea what was going on. She wanted to think of a cool way to react to the situation. Were they making fun of her? Was this a test? Was Kitty having a breakdown?

"What's going on?" Jane said finally, when Kitty stopped and knelt at Jane's feet. She was moving her head around slowly with the mask on as if she were in some sort of a trance. Jane looked up at Kitty's friends. "What the fuck?"

They ignored Jane and collected their things, pausing on their way out of the change room.

"Come on, Kitty cat," a girl named Amber who was known to have parties in her parents' basement said. Maybe the party they were talking about was going to be at Amber's.

Kitty got up and left with them. She was still wearing the mask. Her plan could have been to wear it for the rest of the day around school. Jane didn't know. She started to cry.

She continued to dress herself, fumbling to pull her pants over both legs with shaking hands. She felt the kind of soft body tremor that turns into a jolt, one that comes with any sort of violation. It occurred to her that she was being bullied—a strong word—by someone who was a complete loser, purring like a cat on the dirty floor of a high school change room. Years later it would occur to Jane that Kitty was on drugs.

The café where they meet for the first time outside their mutual work shifts is a popular one, full of calculated outfits and grown-out haircuts. It's clear the owners have done their best to pack in as many tables as they can so they seat more people and make more money. Jane already tried to get up to go to the bathroom but immediately sat back down when she noticed her crotch was in the face of the person at the table beside her. They noticed and their attention made Jane wonder if her crotch smelled bad. Jane wants to ask Kitty what she thinks of the middle part she's tried out this morning.

"What are you doing?" Kitty makes an expression that Jane hasn't seen yet but will come to know well, laughter mixed with contempt, mostly conveyed through the widening of her large eyes.

Soon it's Kitty's turn to go to the bathroom. Before she gets up, she faces the table next to them. "I'm about to get in your face."

Her wording strikes Jane as strange. What's more, Jane notices that Kitty has something that she doesn't—a brilliant smile. It makes her wonder if it's better to have nice eyes or a nice smile. Kitty has both. Everyone laughs and they shuffle their table over.

But Kitty's not done. "Would you rather have my ass or my crotch in your face?"

Jane would smile but she doesn't want to. When Kitty is gone, she gets up to refill both of their plastic cups with water. It's safe for her to move now that their neighbours have pulled the table farther away. Like most places in Toronto there is a stand with cups and jars filled with tap water. The cups remind her of the ones that are given to toddlers so that they don't hurt themselves—colourful plastic that won't shatter if thrown on the floor. Some of Kitty's coral lipstick gets on Jane's finger while she's filling her blue cup with stale, warm water.

"You look like Andy Warhol."

Jane turns around to see a middle-aged man grinning stupidly at her as if he has just seen the most hilarious thing.

"Pardon?"

"With your hair like that and the thick black glasses." He's referring to Jane's reading glasses, which she had been wearing before Kitty arrived and forgotten about. A low prescription earning her the scorn of people who wear glasses and contacts every day.

"Oh."

He turns to the person next to him. "Doesn't she look like Andy Warhol?" he asks. He's still laughing.

"I don't know, I guess?" The onlooker shrugs and looks down at their phone.

Jane doesn't like the comparison. Not for any particular reason other than the man's tone and the tangible desperation in his laughter. She doesn't know why she cares. She feels like she's floating as she makes her way back to the small table. Kitty still hasn't returned.

Jane takes this opportunity to look around—mostly at what shoes everyone is wearing. There's a lot of Converse, white high-tops. Some sandals, but mostly sneakers that are all impeccably clean. She wants to ask everyone how they keep them that way. Everyone around her is pretty beautiful. No one is wearing much makeup. No one is wearing a bra. The man who told her she looks like Andy Warhol is older than everyone here. He's staring at her, raising his eyebrows as if he expects her to walk over and start talking to him, as if her attention could save him from something. This will not be the case.

"You took ages," Jane states plainly before she remembers to smile at Kitty.

"I was doing a line."

Jane has no idea if she's joking. Of coke? It would be weird for Jane to continue talking to her assuming it's coke in case it isn't coke. This could be a terrible, friendship-ending mistake.

"Jealous." This seems like a safe thing for Jane to say.

"I know it's a bit much for the middle of the day."

"It's cool. I'd do it too if I had any."

"Go, take a bump."

"Okay."

With a new confidence, Jane shuffles through the small gap between the two tables and leans in close to Kitty, who covers Jane's hand with both of hers, leaving Jane with a little baggie.

Jane pauses for a beat. Thinking about whether or not she should thank this gorgeous person who is about to become her friend.

"Don't hesitate!" Kitty yells, drawing attention to them both. Kitty returns her gaze to the table next to her and smiles at them. "Don't!" They laugh.

Jane always feels like she's going to get caught, no matter how many times she does it. She nestles her hands deep into the pockets of her jeans and cups them around her protruding hip bones. While walking down the stairs to the washroom, she checks to see if anyone is watching her and wonders where she would put the coke if someone came with the intention to search her. Maybe she would swallow it all. Maybe she'd put it inside her pussy.

The restroom is disgusting. Jane looks at herself in a mirror that has a thick film over it, making it difficult to see her own reflection as she plays around with the part of her hair in an attempt to make herself look less like Andy Warhol. The mirror looks like it's been steamed from a shower. Someone has managed to rub an outline of a dick into the residue. Possibly an employee. If she were a more secure person, the Andy Warhol comment would not have bothered her. She could just take off her glasses.

In the stall, there is barely any room for her to move. The baggie has little pictures on it but they are faded and Jane can't make them out. She forgot to bring something to snort it or cut it with. She can use the house keys in her pocket even though that strikes her as gross. She wipes the key with toilet paper before she does it, aware that what she is doing is futile.

Walking back to their table, Jane watches Kitty's exaggerated arm movements as she chats with their neighbours. Her congeniality is starting to annoy Jane, someone with limited emotional resources who doesn't care to make any conversational or emotional investment in someone she is never going to see again. The coke will work soon. That could help. Jane could come across as dull if she doesn't try and talk to these people.

"Some guy told me I look like Andy Warhol with these glasses." Jane shrugs as she sits down with the new group that's formed. They stop talking and study Jane. Concentration shows on their faces as if they are taking this moment and their response to it very seriously. Maybe they don't know if Andy Warhol is cool or not. Maybe they want to try and say the right thing.

"You sort of do," someone at the other table says.

"Who said it?" Kitty asks.

"Over there, but don't all look." Jane nods her head backwards in the direction of the man who she assumes is still staring and smiling at her, unless he has anything better to do.

"Maybe you should tell him you're actually Valerie Solanas." Kitty smiles.

The coke is kicking in and Jane wants to go. She doesn't want to be alone, though, and she hopes that Kitty will want to do something other than sit here with these people.

"What are you doing after this?" Jane asks Kitty directly, ignoring everyone else. She's half-worried that Kitty will ask them along.

"No plans. Maybe I'll go home to cry and masturbate." At this everyone nods in an exaggerated way that Jane assumes is meant to be taken as knowing. Kitty is grinding her teeth. This small discomfort of Kitty's relieves Jane for many reasons but mostly because it means the coke is good. She wants more. If she can incorporate Kitty giving her more coke into their plans, things will be grand.

The occupants of the table next to them lose interest. They are now poring over someone's phone with a general, subdued laughter.

"Wanna go to the museum?" Jane asks Kitty.

"Why?"

"To look at the sparkling rocks."

"There are sparkling rocks?"

"Yeah, like a whole room of them."

"That honestly sounds kind of cool."

"It's not bad."

"Is it expensive?"

"I have a pass that will get us both in for free."

"Sure, I have nothing better to do." Kitty says.

Jane stands up and undoes the mini-backpack she has strung around the back of her seat to check for her phone and wallet. Kitty is carrying a canvas tote bag as a purse which is what everyone does around here. The tote bag is important, and it says a lot about a person. The pressure of picking an appropriate tote bag is too much for Jane. That's why she's gone with the leather backpack. Kitty's tote is black with a scientific photo of a bat skeleton. It's perfect.

As they make their way out of the café, the table they were chatting with wave and yell goodbye to Kitty. They are all very excited. It is going to be a wonderful day.

"We can take the subway," Jane says, pointing down the street. She lets Kitty take the lead to the entrance, down the stairs. She walks fast, like her. Jane notices that Kitty already has her card out, ready to tap. She appreciates her efficiency.

"We should have done another bump before we left." Kitty sighs. The subway halls are empty enough for them to walk side by side.

"They have bathrooms there." Once they reach the platform, a flashing sign informs Jane that the eastbound train is due in a minute.

"I went on a date with a guy who used to love fucking in the museum bathroom," Kitty says. "He and I never got there, though; he would just tell me all the time that he loved it."

"You didn't want to?"

"I probably would have if it ever came down to it."

"Like, if you made a plan to go fuck."

"Yeah, I guess I wasn't ready for a lot of the stuff he wanted to do."

"I get what you mean."

"It's embarrassing. I'm into stuff like that now." The train glides towards them.

"Stuff like that?" Jane asks while they climb on. Kitty points to a couple of empty seats and they nestle themselves across from a couple who are organizing multiple square shopping bags full of new clothing.

"You know what I mean," Kitty says. Jane can only guess. It's the same risk as earlier, when Jane was afraid to assume Kitty had coke.

"Maybe you just weren't there yet." Again, a safe thing for Jane to say. Honest enough to imply some sort of emotional risk without forming any opinion or giving anything away.

"It was nice out. We should have walked," Kitty replies dreamily.

Kitty starts to hum a song to herself while nodding her head frenetically. Jane says nothing for a moment. When their stop is announced, Jane heads to the nearest exit but is startled by a cry. She turns around while hovering her hand near the door to prevent it from closing. Kitty has tripped on something and fallen over. She lies on her back on the floor of the subway, making a grand gesture of her mistake like a soccer player who stays down on the field after being hit by another player. Kitty's smile is still quite brilliant, even on the grimy floor of a Toronto subway car. There is a humility in it all.

Jane releases her hand from the door.

Kitty is by now surrounded by a number of concerned passengers. Although everyone is worried, Jane wants it to be clear that she is the most important person to Kitty. She pushes through the people who are surrounding Kitty as the car starts moving again. They will get off at the next stop.

"You okay?" Jane places her arms under Kitty's to help her up.

"Yeah, I tripped over his feet." Kitty points down the hallway of the subway car at no particular person.

"All right. We'll get off here?"

"Yeah, I'm good."

The line at the museum is short and it doesn't take long for them to get tickets printed, which seems like a bit of a waste to Jane. The tickets get scanned at the entrance right beside the desk, meaning that it takes about four seconds to walk there. Why even print them? Can't they all just shout at each other who's shown a pass? She wants to express these thoughts to Kitty but feels nervous and a bit high. Maybe Kitty will get bored of her soon. She's still shocked they're even here. Entering the gallery, Jane focuses on slow breathing as well as a flood of affirmations that don't stay in her brain long enough to resonate. Things like "this is hilarious, who cares," "she's with you because she wants to be," and "just let her do all the talking." They enter a large hall lined with various animal skeletons.

"Where are the sparkling rocks?" Kitty's voice is quite high, and it is enough to echo throughout the hall. She begins to skip across the floor—a gesture that seems out of character for her. Jane isn't about to start skipping. That would be ridiculous. Kitty does manage to pull it off, though.

Jane picks up the pace of her walk to catch up.

"The rocks are this way." She points to a large staircase. A mosaic of stained glass enters into Jane's peripheral—a beautiful gallery ceiling. She wants to take a photo of it. Jane is reluctant to take photos in front of someone she doesn't know well and wants to impress. It's risky. Kitty could think she's simple if she chooses the wrong thing.

"Do you have a roommate?" Jane wants to hide the fact that she's panting as they climb the stairs.

"Nope."

"Me neither."

"How do you not have a roommate?" Kitty says.

"I asked you first."

"My parents pay for some of it, as long as I work."

"At the Fish Bar?"

Kitty smiles. "I show up there from time to time."

"I live in a basement," Jane mutters in a dark tone as if she resents being there. But really, she's grateful for the basement and happy to be alone—not that she ever really is with Richard there, or Vronsky. Basements are a bit of a mind-fuck, unless you're depressed already. If you're so depressed that living in a basement without much sun couldn't possibly make anything worse, then being there is fine.

Kitty props herself on a bench once they reach the top of the stairs. Jane isn't positive she won't pull out a cigarette and light it right inside the museum. For some reason she feels like if Kitty did that she would follow suit—light one up herself. They sit for a moment, high on coke and excited to see the precious gems, rare gold specimens, crystals, whatever anyone wants to call them.

"The sparkling rocks." Kitty is speaking with urgency.

"Yes, they are very important."

four

Kitty gets promoted to manager at the Fish Bar. She and Jane have hung out a few times since their trip to the museum, which ended with them doing more coke in the bathroom and taking pictures of each other posing near displays of medieval Germanic helmets.

Kitty asks Jane to sweep the shack while Jane has an extraordinary number of tables.

"Fuck off." Jane brushes by Kitty and starts to punch in orders. Jane was already feeling exhausted when the evening rush started. But she has nothing to complain about. Jane might be reacting to Kitty because she has nothing better to do while she waits for her table's food to be ready.

"We're out of calamari," someone yells from the kitchen. Jane can't make out if it's one of her pals.

"Jesus Christ."

"I could fire you," Kitty says. "You're drunk every day."

Jane is struck by her tone. "Can you go tell every table I have that they're not getting their fucking gross calamari?"

"This isn't about the calamari. You're drunk."

"Chill. I do what I need to do."

"Are you on the sambuca again?"

"Sambuca is gross," Jane says. "Where are you getting that from?"

"I used to steal it from my parents in high school. They love it." Kitty pauses while she fixes the bun on top of her head, taking a bobby pin and placing it in her mouth, maintaining eye contact with Jane all the while. Jane no longer cares if anyone gets their calamari. Kitty takes the bobby pin out of her mouth and pushes it inside her hair bun. Jane isn't sure what the pin is doing, if it's helping. Kitty points her finger beyond Jane to another table of men who are waving frantically in an attempt to get her attention. Jane walks over to take their order.

She finds it odd that Kitty would dredge up high school. Once again, Jane is back in the change room watching Kitty's ridiculous spectacle. A moment of flippant cruelty. Now they do coke in the museum together. They even almost had their first fight. In the present, their friendship feels tenuous and flirtatious in a way that reminds Jane of Richard. A whimsical force that makes her feel good. One that could come and go at any moment. Jane doesn't really think of high school much, but her past interactions with Kitty are unconsciously present, in the way that someone might feel a small thrill after stealing something trivial.

That night while doing their cash-outs, Kitty and Jane sit across from each other. They chat uselessly about the customers they hated. All of them. Kitty mentions a bald man who asked for her phone number while his wife was in the washroom. No one ever asks Jane for her phone number.

"He said he wanted to take my photograph," Kitty sneers.

"He your type?" Jane doesn't know Kitty's preference for a partner. She appears to lack the paralyzing neurosis that Jane has, allowing her to exude the impulsive sexuality of someone who knows they will forget anything they say or do in a minute. She often braids her long black hair while she is concentrating on something like counting money, letting the braid fall apart once she's figured it out. Jane catches herself staring at Kitty, wondering how she could be so attractive. She has an unusually large mouth.

Kitty lets out a breath and smiles the sarcastic half-smile that brings Jane a surprising amount of comfort. Then, Kitty's face grows cold.

"I'm missing one hundred dollars."

"How do you know?" They work hard in excruciating heat, and losing money would suck for anyone. She will help Kitty look for it.

"I got an American hundred from some tourists and it's gone."

"Are you sure?"

"I'm positive. You were also the only one close enough to steal it."

"What?" The accusation sobers Jane.

Kitty grabs all her money in one hand, stomping away from the table, turning back only to grab her phone that she's left. It's protected by a sparkling black case that makes it look like it's covered in dewdrops. As she dials, she stuffs her cash into the little black pouch that's still tied around her waist. Jane doesn't know why Kitty left the table. If it was to get away from her, it hasn't worked. Kitty has moved only a few feet away to yell into her phone—presumably with the owner, who has gone home for the night—about how someone stole her money, staring at Jane with dark, narrowed eyes. Jane wants to comfort her. She's startled by this harsh shift in her mood, and this switch resonates with Jane as a confirmation that their friendship was too good to be true. Still, Jane isn't ready to be accused of stealing. She pushes her own money into her pouch, puts the pouch inside the mini-backpack that she brought with her to work, and rises from the table to join Kitty.

"I would never take your money."

"Who else would have?"

"I have my own."

When money goes missing at the Fish Bar, employees involved need to attend a hearing, but what that really means is that Jane and Kitty have to go to work early on the day of their respective shifts and have a smoke with the owner of the restaurant, telling their story about what they think happened.

Jane will come to learn that Kitty told everyone she wouldn't work with Jane. They had to choose to keep Jane or her.

"So, Kitty quit?" Jane asks a couple days later, after not seeing her on the schedule.

"We don't do ultimatums here." The owner of the Fish Bar would be attractive if not for his paunch and his stench, a mixture of fried fish and cigarette smoke.

Jane phones Kitty a few times in the next two days, her motivation being to clear her name as well as check that Kitty is doing okay. Richard keeps making jokes about it—prodding her to admit she actually stole the cash. They laugh but Jane is concerned about Kitty's health. She'd been caught up in her own ego while they both went through their hearings, pissed off that she had been accused. She doesn't make as much through tips as Kitty because Jane is rude and absent-minded at work. But whether Jane realizes it or not, she's accepted this penchant for dissociation. Whatever skills she lacks as a server wouldn't be enough to motivate her to steal. Everyone who works at the restaurant believes Jane. Their faith in her is comforting and almost feels like a win, despite the circumstances. It is possibly the only time she has managed to be more relatable and trustworthy than Kitty. Their confidence in her is compelling but this doesn't stop her from selectively forgetting to ring in food items so she can make double the "tips," as if she is fulfilling her destiny as a thief. It's something she feels she deserves because of the emotional pain that the Fish Bar has brought into her life.

Jane is in bed masturbating and when that's over she dials Kitty's number again, expecting nothing. There is no correlation between the two things. She just thinks it's easier to try and save this friendship than to try and make a new friend. To Jane's delight and possible exhaustion, Kitty picks up. Jane has no idea how this will go.

"Hi, Jane." Her sucrose voice blends her curt answer into something that makes Jane forget how annoyed she is with everything about her.

"Kitty, come on."

"You need the money for coke."

"I don't."

"I almost miss working there. Mostly the extra cash."

"What can I do to make this better?"

"We're cool. I just wanted you to admit it."

Admit what? Jane chooses to remain silent.

———

Since she suspects Richard has been cheating on her, Jane has decided this is the last time she will let him into her bed. As they lie together, she pulls her head closer to his cold body. Over the past weeks she's seldom heard from him and has received cryptic texts complimenting her big lips and gorgeous smile. They were meant for someone else.

Jane can't prove her theory about Richard's texts. All she knows is her smile doesn't fit the bill. Her lips are tiny. She's considered getting injections, but Richard doesn't want her to. He claims that the lip augmentation will just deflate when she goes to give him a blow job. Jane isn't sure what the science behind that would be. She doesn't ask. Instead, she feels guilty because the fact that Richard said that makes her like him more.

And what of this possessiveness? Their casual fucking or whatever intimacy they have sometimes seems like more of a friendship—or a necessity. Jane consistently wants someone else. Richard must want someone else, too.

"How does it feel to be the most handsome man in the room?" Jane asks him.

"I wouldn't know, ask Burt Reynolds."

"I think I have a concussion. My head feels like there is a giant clamp over it."

"It's your antidepressants," he answers flatly.

"I think you're fucking Celine Thompson." The woman she is referring to sends him nudes he claims he never asked for. Jane has only seen flashes of the photos before Richard whips his phone out of her sight.

"You have nothing to worry about."

"Just tell the truth." She softens her face.

"Celine Thompson doesn't deserve your wrath."

"You have your new apartment. This is the last time I want you here."

"She's not my type. Seems like a boring lay."

"It's the fact I have to worry."

Richard's face melts into an exaggerated pout then he shrugs. He gives Jane a baggie of coke and says that it's his last gift. He repeats himself, claiming that his cock and the coke are his last gift. Jane doesn't know if she should consider this a breakup, but she wants to tell him about her crush. He lives in the apartment above her and they sometimes interact while she is smoking and he is locking up his bicycle. One time he told her that he liked her sunglasses. He seems well-adjusted—as does his girlfriend.

"I want to fuck this guy who lives above me. We follow each other on Instagram." Jane knows Richard will want to see what he looks like.

"I want to see."

"I'll show you, here." She passes him her phone set on the guy's public profile. The picture shows him holding a blow-up doll in one hand and a can of craft beer with a picture of a cottage on it in the other.

"That's hilarious. He'll never like you."

"Why not?"

"You dress like shit."

"I thought you liked my grunge look."

"What kind of shoes does he wear?" Richard asks.

"I don't know, Vans?"

"Wow."

"What does that mean?"

"What kind of boots do you wear in the winter?"

"Docs?"

"You're wearing the wrong shoes."

"You mean I should be wearing those ugly ones that everyone has?"

"Yeah, you can bet his girlfriend has those."

"Crocs?" Jane is trying to make a joke.

"You're nothing he would take seriously, trust me. Is he a corporate dude?"

"Yeah."

"To him, you're this weird girl."

"I am a bit odd."

"He won't even understand your music."

"I don't make music."

"The techno. You know, the music you listen and dance to."

"I don't think it's that bad."

"He knows he can count on you to tell him where to get coke at three in the morning."

"You know just what to say."

"Looks like you're stuck with me."

"I guess so."

"What's hilarious about this, Jane, is that you're smart and hot, and no one will want to date you because of that."

"I'm not."

"That guy wouldn't even be able to fuck you. He'd come in less than a minute."

"You don't know that."

"It's true. He'd come on your stomach then roll over and fall asleep. You'd have to show him how to fuck you properly, which is impossible because you can't be fucked properly by someone who doesn't already know."

Jane pauses. She wants to say something clever, but she knows that Richard is right. Maybe there are just people who have been through things and people who haven't. She feels like she has seen the true darkness of life somehow, even though she is just like every other person. Maybe she is just a young person who has felt the smallest bit of sadness.

"Richard?"

"Yeah?"

"Can we do chair time?"

"Not now. I have to go find an amp for Scotty. Goodnight!"

Jane doesn't know why he's saying goodnight. It's five in the afternoon. He still has to get dressed to leave her apartment, and it would have made more sense if he'd said goodnight on his way out the door. She buries her face in her pillow—willing him to leave so she can just drink or get stoned or both.

He continues, "These corporate dudes, they're not in touch with reality. They don't understand a good thing when they see it. A good thing like you."

"I thought I was a weird girl who dresses like shit."

"You are." Richard gets out of bed and starts to search for his clothes on the floor. He pulls on a larger version of Jane's own favourite black shirt. He starts to put on a pair of her black jeans until he realizes that they're not his. Then he finds his own. The ones with the cigarette burn near the knee.

"That's why you're stuck with me, like I said. I'm the only one who understands you. It's you and me forever."

"I thought your cock was my last gift."

"And the coke!" It is time for Richard to do the thing that she loves most about him. He smiles, not at her but to himself. The cruelty comes out in his eyes and mouth. He is far away—probably has been for a long time.

Jane believes what he's saying. Richard pulls on one of his socks and then finds one of Jane's sparkling blue ones and settles for that. He heads towards the door, which is a relief to Jane.

"Goodnight!"

Jane sits up. "Richard, wait one second!"

"What?"

"I dreamt about the northern lights."

"Recently?"

"I don't know. I was in Iceland on a boat."

"Would love to talk about this. Another time."

"Really?"

"I'm leaving!"

Jane doesn't understand the concept of codependency yet—what they get from each other. How this pattern even exists. Sometimes she feels like she isn't enough, and that Richard is getting nothing from her, but more often she is left wondering if he needs her attention, or if he feels like he wants to teach her something. It will take a long time for her to understand the patterns of callous older men.

Jane spends four days in bed staring at the disco ball Richard put above it one drunken night. She dreams about the northern lights again, but the dream doesn't make sense because she has never witnessed them in real life. Although, she feels like she has a body-memory of the feeling of seeing something magical in the sky that is sought-after, something people pay to see. She's weeping, in the dream.

Richard had spent a long time trying to get the disco ball to stay, mostly by making a hole in the ceiling with a nail. Then he pulled a little hook out of his pocket and screwed it in the hole he'd just made. The disco ball was about the size of a basketball and mostly made of sequins and Styrofoam. If it fell, it wouldn't kill Jane.

On the fifth morning, she puts makeup on and takes a selfie sitting up on her bed. She chooses a discreet filter that makes it look like she isn't using a filter at all. For the photo's caption, she writes: *alone*. Richard comments: *We'll be friends again soon*. Jane deletes the comment, then the photo. He seems unaffected by their breakup. Maybe they have only broken up in Jane's head. She wishes that he would contact her with some sort of apology so that she, in turn, could tell him that he is a fuckass.

Jane notices a text from her boss reminding her about the afternoon shift she's booked for. Jane sets an alarm on her phone and goes back to sleep, planning to take some coke before her shift starts because the nap will do more bad than good. It could make her drowsy.

When she walks into the restaurant, she's told she has three tables that have just been seated and are waiting for her to take their drink orders. The owner pleads with her to hurry and get "ready to perform" even though she's thirty minutes early. One of the other servers hasn't shown up for their shift.

Jane doesn't feel like she owes her colleagues anything, so she takes her time changing into her black dress and flats in the shack. She checks to see if anyone is around and does a line out of her locket necklace. She emerges with a fresh, enthusiastic smile—working diligently until she wants another boost. Later, in the bathroom, she sends a message to Anna: *Shifts at the Fish Bar are a lot more fun on cocaine.* Anna replies that Jane must be present, but Jane doesn't understand what that could possibly mean.

In hour seven of her shift, Jane hits the wall and knows she's had too many shots that she's been convincing tables to buy her, on top of the cocaine. She has to leave. She transfers her tables to a server who has just arrived and feigns sunstroke. Something she's already done with the owner once this year.

"I get tired in the sun."

"Do you need a hat? What did you do last night?"

"I'm going to pass out. Do you want a fainting employee on your hands?"

"You look like you're burning up."

"Thank you."

On her way home Jane starts to aggressively clean out her purse. There is a hole in the lining that catches her attention. She digs her hand in, tracing the lining of the purse with two fingers until she can feel something crumpling between her fingers. Jane feels a mixture of shock and sickness as she unfolds the American hundred. Did she steal it and not remember? She stuffs it back into the lining while fighting off tears. The taxi driver asks if she is okay.

———

A year ago, Anna packed up and moved to Toronto from the small southwestern Ontario town where she and Jane grew up in different generations. Anna was quiet about the details of her nervous breakdown and brief stay in an institution, following the loss of her psychotherapist's license and the fight for custody of her daughter. She recounted the story to Jane when they first met for coffee in the city right after her move. Anna spoke in a subdued tone, as if the memory was a bad dream Anna herself didn't fully understand.

Anna hadn't taken the fact that she'd lost her practice lightly. She'd managed to gain custody of Gracie because of her ex-husband's indifference but, after a few failed relationships, had grown to resent her child, crediting the poor thing as the source of her misfortune. She was beautiful, with olive skin that stayed sort of nice forever, but eventually her desperation for companionship seeped into her outer appearance. The creases in her forehead deepened when she sighed, which was often. Her letdowns cumulated in despair. She began to abuse her ex-husband's leftover pain medication from four years prior. Ten-year-old Gracie ran away and was found sleeping in the neighbour's shed. Anna lost custody, forcing her estranged ex-husband to take their daughter in. Jane feels sad for Anna. She sees her as a cautionary tale. They spent a day together on the Toronto Island right after it happened. They mostly spoke about what was going on around them—all the different smells of the budding trees after winter. How the island is such a nice escape from the city.

Anna works as a psychic now. She has told Jane she likes the work. Anna needed time away from the reminders of her previous life. Although she doesn't have any psychic abilities like clairvoyance, levitation, or telepathy, she gets steady business because she impresses clients with nomenclature from her former life. Her experience as a therapist helps her read their body language and tailor her psychic predictions towards specific needs and desires. It's easy for her to guess how their childhoods went—what their attachment styles are. She's also turned her office into a massage parlour to bring in more money.

Anna's office is painted a glossy blue-violet that reflects the silver neon lights in the window. When Jane enters, she's asked to take her shoes off by a tall woman wearing a lot of red eyeshadow who looks about her age. Jane hesitates because she knows that a terrible stench will lead to her if she removes her work shoes. She passes by the woman and nods timidly as she lets herself into a separate room to see Anna.

"Richard has left me," Jane declares. She makes a show of fainting into the leather armchair in front of the desk where Anna sits. Anna opened this place with some sort of small business grant which she used to buy crystals and copies of every tarot deck in existence, including an *Alice in Wonderland* one. The decks of cards lie neatly on a glass display shelf on the far wall of her office.

"Dry your tears." Anna lights an oil lamp while using her other hand to search inside a drawer under her desk. Jane notes that she is not, nor does she feel like, crying.

Sometimes Jane wonders if the tragedy of Anna's life matches her beauty, which one is stronger. It's midnight, the time Anna usually gets busy with crowds of drunk people coming during their nights out. She put some money into decorating the outside lobby of the place so that it works well for Instagram photos—pictures are only allowed outside, though. The smell of the oil burning reminds Jane of pine needles, like when there would be a Christmas tree at home. She wonders if Anna will get one here.

Still fumbling inside the drawer, Anna gives out a sigh and says, "I always lose the remote for these damn lights." Then she says, "Ta-da," pulling out a small grey remote.

"You can sometimes get lights that you can control with an app from your phone." Jane regrets saying that immediately because she doesn't know if Anna can afford such a thing and also because she doesn't feel like explaining smart home applications to her. In frames from Dollarama, there are pictures of Anna with various celebrities Photoshopped in—their faces now dull ghosts under the varying flicker of the oil lamp.

"How can I dry my tears when I cannot cry?"

"He was attracted to you because of your vulnerability."

"My vulnerability?"

"Richard will return to show you." Before Jane can ask what she means, Anna gets up and sways through a doorway with a velvet curtain.

five

Even after starting art school in the fall, Jane doesn't want to make any friends who are not Kitty. There's a point in every semester where a cut-off happens. In the middle of the fall, everyone is already clinging to people who will get them through the rest of the school year.

Their first semester has two seminars per week, each based on a certain topic. Their class of twenty students discusses things like theory, aesthetics, museum studies, history of art, performance, art around the world, entrepreneurship for creatives, curation practices, and where they will go out to drink after class. She and Kitty sit in the far corner of the room close to the door because Jane often leaves the room without realizing it to go to the bathroom and look at herself in the mirror. Outside of the seminars, they're provided with their own private studios on campus, but they rarely go.

"How did we get in?" Jane genuinely feels like she was accepted by mistake. She's languid and irritable. Her hangovers equate everyday living and fighting. Her peers are already coming up with brilliant installations, sculptures and digital art, while she can't decide whether painting Amy Winehouse is a good or bad idea.

"I know why I got in." Kitty's smug. "Do you?"

Kitty's application was a link to a YouTube video of her sitting in front of a webcam apologizing for embarrassing shit she's seen other people do. Kitty isn't uncomfortable about anything. She told Jane she wore a pink cheerleader uniform and had someone do a light installation that made it look like she was at a rave. It sounds somewhat boring when Jane describes it to people. You'd have to see it to understand, Jane tells people at parties because she would rather describe her friend's art than her own. The video was titled *Consolation Prize for a Genius (Truth)*. Jane feels as though she, herself, is different. Her childhood bullying and isolation have led her into the throes of a vicious inferiority complex. The damage she's done to her nervous system doesn't help her ability to stay outside of her own home for long periods of time. In fact, Jane's paranoia allows her to interpret the subtle flick of a stranger's eyelids as a direct personal attack.

She notices delicate aesthetic differences between the way people at her school dress. No one is wearing skinny jeans anymore. Jane doesn't want to give them up. No one is wearing knee socks. She can't give those up either. Her colleagues maintain highly stylized and aesthetically beautiful social media pages like well-adjusted people.

When Jane is with Kitty she gets a sort of contact high, like she could possibly be brilliant too, or she has at least tricked a brilliant person into hanging out with her. She wonders how much shared interests can bond people, just a couple of servers, just a couple of drinkers. When they go out together Kitty almost serves as Jane's bridge to the world. People who normally wouldn't have talked to her suddenly do.

"What about a Winehouse tribute?" Jane peeks her head out of the bathroom in her apartment while she sits on the toilet. She's wondering if pissing while talking to Kitty will put her off. Their friendship quickly evolved from supporting each other through their shitty jobs to their museum trip to hanging out all the time. Their fight about the money seems to be resolved, bringing them a bit closer, although Jane is unsure what lesson to take from the whole situation. Now they're collaborating on an art project to submit as an application for a travel grant from their university.

"You know, people romanticize her lifestyle but it's actually quite sad," Kitty says.

"People romanticize her dying?"

"Yes, things like the 27 Club—you know," Kitty replies, impatiently.

"Why did she die?"

"Why does anyone die, Jane?"

"How?"

"She died of an overdose."

"Interesting—of what?" Jane knows exactly how Amy Winehouse died but it feels good to hear it again for some reason.

Kitty's on the floor painting her nails a carrot colour that won't match any of her clothes. Jane doesn't warn Kitty that her nails look like shit, as they've recently fought about Jane's ennui.

"You're kind of, like, negative," Kitty had said.

"Oh."

They stopped talking for a few days but then Kitty called her like nothing had happened to tell her an extraordinary story about how she got drunk and almost went home with the owner of the Fish Bar.

They'd gone shopping together once and Jane felt like they were on a first date—or that Kitty was conducting a thorough job interview. Maybe because there was no coke that time. Kitty seemed keen on asking Jane questions and opinions on spectacular made-up circumstances, but mostly things about her social presence online:

"Do you care about your follower-to-following ratio?"

"Do you share the results of a story poll after it's over?"

"Do you delete a photo if not enough people have liked it?"

"Is your account private?"

Jane answered all her questions with tact. She doesn't care about the follower ratio, she only uses the platform for close friends, mostly because the internet kind of scares her and she's worried that she will embarrass herself. She sometimes shares the story poll but usually forgets.

This all comes out as "I don't take myself too seriously—I'm boring!"

While the exchange took place, Kitty was inside a change room trying on marked-up vintage clothes comparable to items Jane could find at Value Village if she searched hard enough. Kitty dragged the curtain open and it made a loud screeching noise that startled Jane. She was smoothing her hair down. There was a pile of black clothing strewn on a chair in front of the mirror into which Kitty stared.

Jane had a childhood friend who was very beautiful in a way that attracted a lot of attention. Most of the time, Jane would go to Hannah's house to play because they were neighbours. Hannah would be flaunting some exquisite new toy that her parents had bought her.

One day when Jane rang Hannah's doorbell, her mom answered and pointed one of her long fingers painted with a nail polish called "Oxblood." Jane knew this because Hannah had once stolen it only so she could use it in front of Jane, painting her nails silently and without error. Jane looked where Hannah's mother was pointing. She walked across the street.

Hannah was driving a plastic pink convertible with a tiny motor made for children. Her pigtails were sticking directly out of either side of her head. Like her mother, Hannah had an agent, because she was paid to model children's clothing in Sears catalogues. She'd often show Jane pictures of herself wearing the nicest clothes. The clothes she was wearing looked like they were made for women, giving Jane the impression that Hannah was playing dress-up. Hannah's family was wealthy, even having procured Hannah tickets to see the Spice Girls in the fall. She always liked to brag about things that she was doing, and she never let Jane drive her convertible.

"Hey."

"Hey, Jane." Hannah waved but did not stop steering her car. She started driving in circles around Jane.

Jane had wanted to talk to Hannah about a book she was reading, *The Lion, the Witch and the Wardrobe*. It was something about one of the witches casting a mean spell that would make one of the children always too hot or always too cold. Well, it was something like that. Jane struggled to remember the details of the witch's cruelty, but the thought of the spell happening to her had left her frightened. She'd gone to her parents' bedroom late at night after reading it, convinced that the witch was going to come and cast a spell on her and that she somehow deserved it.

Jane went to her father's side of the bed and pushed on his arm with one hand to wake him up. She held the book in the other. "I'm scared of the witch."

"What witch?"

"The witch in the book." She handed him the book with the page about the spell open, as she'd bookmarked it with her finger.

Her father turned on the light.

"I'm trying to sleep," said her mother.

Her father skimmed the page.

"What is she on about?" her mother asked as if Jane wasn't there.

"It seems that the witch in the book has cast a nasty spell." Her father closed the book and motioned for Jane to come in for a hug. "Darling, the witches aren't real. There is no one who can cast a spell on you."

"Jane, please go to bed," her mother added.

Jane felt no comfort. She left their room and returned to her bed, thinking of ways that she could try and be good so that such a thing would never happen.

She wanted to tell all of this to Hannah, as if Hannah could support her parents' theory about the existence of the witch. "I read this book about a bunch of children and a witch."

Hannah continued to ride around her in her convertible, not acknowledging anything that Jane was saying to her. Then she stopped the car abruptly. The small machine skidded along the sidewalk and its back wheels flew up high, knocking Hannah out of the convertible and onto the ground. She had a few tiny pebbles of gravel on her face when she looked up at Jane, right before she began to cry.

"My shoot! My shoot!" she screamed through sobs.

Jane didn't know what to do. She walked over to Hannah and tried to help her off the road, but she wouldn't move. She went over to the convertible and looked at it, taking in all that it represented to her. It was a symbol of Hannah's constant superiority. She also felt protective towards Hannah, who was still crying beside her. The convertible was upside down with all four wheels spinning and it made Jane think of a bug flipped on its back. She tilted her head to the side and studied the car. Then she wound her right foot behind her and kicked it.

Jane felt her body propel itself backwards and she landed on the small of her back before she felt any pain in her foot.

A car stopped and a woman got out. There was a dog panting out of the passenger window—a golden retriever with a pink collar that had little white paw prints on it. Jane focused on the dog while the woman took in the situation. A plastic convertible, pink and upside down. Two crying children. Maybe the woman thought they'd been fighting over it.

"Where do you live?"

"My shoot! It's tomorrow!" Hannah was wiping pebbles off her face. They left little red spots. She kept crying.

"Over there," Jane said, pointing to Hannah's house with her left pinky finger and hiding her face with the palm of her right hand.

The woman walked across the road in the direction Jane was pointing. When she reached the house, she turned around and motioned to Hannah's front door. Jane gave her a thumbs up then watched her talk to Hannah's mom. Hannah's mom was wearing a white tennis skirt and a tank top. The women walked briskly towards the two girls.

"Is your face okay?" Hannah's mom bent over while keeping her hands on her knees, as if she was studying a freshly baked cake.

"I don't know. Will it be okay for tomorrow?"

"Let's get you inside."

Hannah and her mom left and Jane watched the other woman turn the convertible right side up.

"You okay, dear?" she asked.

"I'm fine," Jane whispered and nodded while she stood up. The woman got back in her car and waited for Jane to wheel the convertible back to the sidewalk. Jane got in the convertible and started to drive.

By watching and sticking close to Kitty, Jane wants to learn how to conduct herself. She's felt null since Richard left.

Jane has a face that rests in permanent disgust but she sometimes remembers this and smiles tightly to appear friendly.

The left wall of Jane's apartment has many framed paintings that she found in Value Village. The walls are also peppered with Lucian Freud paintings that she prints during her rare visits to her parents' house because she refuses to spend valuable drug money on home decor.

"What's that one called?" Kitty asks while pointing at the one with the face and a hand strangling a cat.

"I think it's *Girl with Cat*, or something."

"Oh."

"But what do I know about art!"

"What do we know about the artistes," Kitty says.

The opposite wall is painted with dolls and ballerinas that Jane did herself. It will have to be covered with white paint when she moves out. Beside the ballerinas, there are a series of dark circles like something you would see a possessed child draw in a horror film. They're black and silver. She mostly does them to calm her nerves when coming off drugs. Some of these circles reach up to cover the ceiling.

"How many people have painted Amy?" Jane asks as she joins Kitty, sitting cross-legged on the hardwood floor. While lying on her stomach, Kitty tears another page from one of the magazines she's brought over.

"Depends where you are in the world."

Jane nods at Kitty's fingers smeared with nail polish after ripping the magazine too soon.

"Fuck," Kitty replies without much emphasis. As she reaches for the bottle of orange polish she pauses, then looks up at Jane. "Where's your remover?"

"In Camden, she's everywhere. Statues and murals—"

"No, the remover."

"Oh, I'll get it for you." Jane fumbles as she gets up, doing an awkward skip on her way around the hall to the bathroom. While she reaches her hand into the cupboard under the sink—trying to feel her way around for the shoebox that holds the nail polish remover along with a variety of other things—she picks up Kitty's voice from the other room, yelling. Annoyed that Kitty won't even wait for her to return to the same room, she yells for Kitty to repeat herself.

"I said, maybe we can paint anything else."

"Or not paint." Jane smiles as she re-enters the room, handing the remover and some cotton pads to Kitty.

"Who cares, I'm getting tired," Kitty says while laying entire pages from the magazine on the hardwood floor, turning it all into an effort to repair her nails.

"She's cool, though, Amy."

"Was." Kitty sniffs the nail polish remover. This reminds Jane of something she would do. It also makes her want vodka.

"We should go to London if we get it," Jane states, emphasizing *we*. Jane has developed an obsession with living in London since Anna told her about the escapades she had there in her early twenties.

"London, eh? I guess it depends how much money it is."

"It's a lot of money."

"Do you have friends there?"

"I know a person who may know some people," Jane exaggerates, thinking of Anna and wondering if she still has contacts from when she lived there in the nineties.

"I think you'll get lost."

"Naturally," Jane responds. A dizzied image takes over where she's asking attractive people for directions and they look at her and sneer. But she would grow accustomed to the city and eventually be able to sneer at tourists herself. This assimilation is her goal.

"My dear"—Kitty's put on a fake British accent that's too posh to be realistic—"can I come?"

Jane would like to contact her younger self in high school with the consolation that the girl who mocked her would eventually need her for something.

"Will there be enough money for both of us?" Kitty asks.

"I think so." Drinking alone would be boring.

———

A week goes by with their usual classes and drinking after them. One night, Kitty and Jane are back in Jane's apartment. Jane is preparing drinks for them both in her kitchen while Kitty waits in the living room.

"Think I'll get fucked tonight?"

Kitty either doesn't hear Jane's question or is choosing not to answer. When Jane returns with a goblet and a purple pint glass from the dollar store, Kitty makes a joke of staring at it as if she is questioning its contents. Jane gives the goblet to Kitty. They drink and apply makeup in a specific way that will make it look like they aren't wearing any. There is a comfortable silence.

"You must behave yourself," Kitty says when she notices Jane refilling her glass.

"Why are we going to a faculty party? They already hate me."

"Nobody cares about you enough to hate you. Remember that."

When they enter the bar, which is just called Thirsty, three of their classmates are seated around a table decorated with a plastic flower in a mason jar as well as a battery-powered candle. Their classmates' expressions show they've been concentrating really hard on something.

"Kitty, can I grab one?" Jane pokes Kitty until she discreetly hands over one of her lorazepam. She doesn't know if it's wise to waste her drugs here with people she doesn't really like.

Jane dry-swallows it. It's not like she has been invited anywhere else.

In walks Professor Nicolas Price, wearing an azure dress shirt with black suspenders, with streaked brown-grey hair. Everyone calls him the silver fox, an unoriginal name for a wildly gorgeous yet rude gentleman. He's won many awards Jane hasn't heard of. She has the suspicion he made them up. He's holding a CBD vape pen.

Jane walks over to the bar and orders a hoppy beer that she doesn't really like so that she'll drink it more slowly. She drops her beer with Kitty who is talking to two other students who have just arrived. People always take Kitty more seriously, probably because of her tragus piercing. Jane wonders what she would look like with one while walking down the stairs to the restroom, which is decorated with old beer casks.

In the bathroom, she sees a serious girl named Valerie Cabrell who is beautiful in her fragility. Pretty much everyone in the program wants to date her. Not just date her but to bring her home with them forever, to assimilate Valerie into their network of family and friends. She has some pills out on the bathroom counter. Impressed by her level of comfort—laying them out on the bathroom counter as if they were at some Miami drug party in the eighties—Jane approaches Valerie. Maybe this will be the moment where she makes a friend other than Kitty.

"Watcha got there?" Jane grimaces at the sound of her saying "watcha."

Valerie's eyes widen. She looks frightened for a moment then her gaze settles into her coveted neutral, above-it-all blankness. "Adderall," she responds, as if Jane doesn't know what that is.

Jane doesn't understand why she's looking at her this way. She smiles at her.

"Can I try one?"

"I don't have that many." Valerie's smile is thin and Jane can almost detect a hint of laughter in her cold eyes, like Valerie has witnessed something she's going to tell everyone later. Jane realizes that the girl is frightened to be seen speaking with her. She must be an oddity within the students of the art program. As Valerie begins a slow walk backwards, Jane tries to compose herself and think of something clever and unforgettable to say to Valerie. She abruptly turns and darts out the door.

It's only ten and Jane has scared someone off.

Jane stares at the mirror to see how average, even innocent, she appears. The other students make her feel inadequate. Isn't she supposed to be having life-changing debates about the effect of the Industrial Revolution on landscape art? Is she capable of having such a conversation? The good news is that Valerie left her drugs.

Upstairs, she orders a whiskey because her interaction

with Valerie was simply too stressful. She watches the bartender pour her shot into a rocks glass then add a little more with a smile. She pays with a ten-dollar bill then heads towards the others, hoping to avoid Valerie. She nestles herself next to Kitty at the table. Nicolas Price is there. Kitty's mouth makes a shadow on the wall as she laughs confidently with a couple other students. Kitty bridges a social gap Jane can't chill out enough to manage herself. She's never really been good at small talk, while Kitty excels at it. Jane's eyes are very wide, and she often forgets what she's looking at. She gets accused of staring. Her friend's social skills and general pragmatism are both foreign and oblique to Jane.

Once Jane's drunk enough, the conversation with Nicolas Price feels stimulating and right. She likes to ask confident-seeming people about their work to see if they brag, are embarrassed, or have the perfect balance by answering deadpan. No one really does anything they want to do for work nowadays. It's a condition they're all in. Incredibly lucky, trying to translate that luck into some sort of job.

"What were you thinking? When you did that performance art piece?" Jane doesn't know if this question comes across as rude, or if she could have asked it in a more intelligent way.

Kitty overhears and shoots her a familiar look that says she's mildly embarrassed by Jane's behaviour, and that she will continue to watch Jane to try and encourage some restraint or consideration for the effect her actions may have on the person who is considered her closest, most trusted confidante. Saying things at parties is hard.

"Which one?" Nicolas sips a martini, which seems like an odd choice for such a dingy pub. It would be better if he was drinking whiskey. Jane feels an unearned bond with anyone who drinks whiskey.

Jane realizes that she doesn't remember any of his work. She knows that she looked it up.

"Your last piece." Jane rolls these words out slowly so she can maintain eye contact and polite attention for as long as possible. She's terrified of sounding dull, which sometimes causes her to not speak at all. At other times this fear confirms itself as she drinks more and more to withstand social situations.

"I was hoping it would represent music and emotions."

"How do you feel about that?" She is becoming over-whelmed. It seems like the music in the bar has become louder, like they have turned up the volume specifically to stress her out and make her drink more. Or there are just too many people—in Jane's head they all know her shame or they know she's a fraud who doesn't belong here. This possibility makes her shake and repeat things people say back to them. She can't hear what he's saying anymore. She's bored. But does she have the right to be bored when she adds nothing and can barely focus? This egotistical angst is strong. The pills aren't working the way she hoped.

"We all need to connect," he says. Then he looks at Jane as if an idea has just come to him.

"It's like . . ." He mentions a performer she's never heard of. When she admits that she doesn't know the artist, he nods and excuses himself, waving a pack of cigarettes in his hand and leaving his CBD pen on the table. Jane picks it up and puts it in her mouth.

She feels jealous of the hilarious conversation Kitty and Valerie Cabrell are engaged in. Valerie creates erotic sculptures from marzipan and Hubba Bubba gum that she chews while getting fucked. It's in her artist statement—her bio. Chewing the gum while she's getting fucked and using it in her art is an important part of her process. When Jane heard this, she knew Valerie was a true genius.

Now drunk, Jane starts talking to the person across from her whose name she doesn't remember—maybe they're some-one's partner. She says that the only reason Valerie gets any work done is because she has unlimited access to Adderall. Spreading that could limit her options for friendship within this program. But Jane already has Kitty. Will any of these people still see each other after it's all over?

Kitty pulls at her earlobe—their special signal in their sacred drunk language—to show Jane that they need to leave. Once they exit the premises it doesn't matter how they behave. They pull on their light trench coats that would match but for the fact that Jane's is black and Kitty's is beige.

The weather is getting cooler at night now. In their trench coats they are free to choose some dive bar, so they can chat and laugh for a few hours until it's time to go home.

On the floor of Jane's room, Kitty fixes strands that have fallen from her cheap yellow heels with a crochet pattern woven into them. They're pretty fucking ugly, or would be on anyone else. She pushes her finger through a hole near the toe then throws the shoe at the wall. She claims she needs to find love at quarter past four and she cannot possibly do so without proper footwear. Jane suggests that Kitty go online and pick the best-looking person she can find. They're tired and drunk. Jane calls dial-a-bottle but no one picks up so she puts the phone on speaker and continues to reach their voicemail. She knows Kitty's about to pass out but Jane wants the satisfaction of getting through. Kitty gets into Jane's bed.

"I have significant artistic goals," she murmurs before she rolls onto her side.

Jane is ready to sleep on her yoga mat with the comfortable blanket. She doesn't want to get into bed with Kitty because she thinks it might freak her out.

It doesn't matter. The yoga mat feels right. At least, it feels like what she deserves in this very moment. Jane feels like she's gained some unnamed emotion when she touches it. Like she's about to make herself come with a vibrator but stops.

Jane doesn't know if the Adderall is wearing off or just kicking in. Paranoia returns and she begins to think she has a multitude of deadly diseases and that she'll die alone. That she'll never see Richard again. That she'll never be good at painting.

Richard has been sending her texts, which she ignores. Tonight, one reads: *You must have lost my number, call me.* She's bothered by the emotional energy it takes to ignore these messages.

The mat is no longer comfortable. Her central nervous system is buzzing as she springs back onto her feet. She finds herself doing something between a leap and a skip to the closet, where she retrieves a canvas she has stretched herself. The corner is falling off. There is some paint there, too. Not colours she would normally choose. That's why they're left over. After this is all set up her attention shifts to the bathroom and she continues her nervous, energetic stride but can't remember why she wanted to go there. She opens the small cupboard under the sink and rummages around. Her face feels dry and she wants to moisturize. Instead, she grabs a package of *Simpsons*-branded bandages.

Sticking the bandages on the canvas with the care and precision of a surgeon is brilliant. Then she begins the loops. Her hands shake and she strokes her brush aggressively. Jane manages a few dark loops with red in between. It reminds her of a painting she learned about from an elderly volunteer at an art gallery; the circles were supposed to represent the abyss, death, or something non-figurative. This abstraction will be the background for her own secret painting.

Jane wakes in a fit of terror. She's decided to take it easy with the booze, meaning drinking nothing since she last saw Kitty a few days ago. The transition isn't going smoothly. Around dinner time, Jane phones her dad. Instead of asking for help, she finds herself screaming over the phone about how he should have told her that she was being filmed her whole life.

"I'm being filmed by everyone."

"You're not important enough to be filmed."

She continues to sob, hurt at what she perceives to be a great betrayal. They talk through FaceTime, so Jane is able to process her panicked face on the screen of the phone while trying to conceal the calming bottle of wine that she is about to open.

"I thought you were my friend," Jane manages to spew out while wiping mucus from her nose with the hand that isn't holding the wine bottle. She knows she can never tell Kitty about her self-diagnosed acute paranoia. There are many things she cannot tell Kitty.

"I don't think people are filming you, darling," her father sighs.

six

Jane habitually looks at the ground while walking. Tonight the pavement hosts rotting banana peels, broken Heineken bottles, and foam containers that once contained sushi. Back when she lived in the suburbs with her parents Toronto seemed alluring, even necessary, but now many aspects of the city disgust her. She rolls her toe through a hole in one of her knee socks that's been irritating her since she left the house.

Morose and on the verge of isolating, Jane phoned Kitty late in the evening. She'd been unable to concentrate on her new painting with the loops and band aids. Eventually she will have to peel them off, or keep them there and tell people about them as if the *Simpsons* characters hidden under coats of paint could add another layer of meaning.

"Hi," is how Kitty always answers.

"Can I come over? We can work."

"Do you have anything? Not that it matters."

"Yeah, booze." Jane held the phone between her shoulder and ear while opening the fridge door. "Not that we need it."

"Have you noticed a higher tolerance?" Kitty sounded surprised by what Jane has noticed about herself for months.

"Yeah. We both need at least a bottle of wine to feel anything."

"I can't be doing this every night, Jane."

"Me neither."

"See you soon."

The shortcut to Kitty's place sends Jane through a filthy alley. She walks behind a bunch of bars where the staff throw their recycling. Most of it escapes the bins. Sometimes she'll notice used condoms and wonder why people even bother if they're fucking in an alleyway, or if they used it elsewhere and someone just held it in their hand after leaving the apartment, then tossed it.

Beside one of the recycling bins, on a pile of soggy leaves and cigarette butts, a girl twitches in the fetal position. Her dress could be made from yarn—tight, blue, and short, but knitted like her grandmother made it for her because she wanted her to look hot. Jane's wearing librarian clothes—a long skirt and grey cardigan. The girl's legs are thin; they look like they could break with a slight exertion.

What would happen to this girl, who's clearly fucked up, if

she left her lying there? Her impulse to ignore the situation is unnerving. Would she be able to sleep if she just kept walking to Kitty's house, pretending not to see? Jane is never afraid to walk through alleys alone.

A man approaches them, waving to someone in the distance. He ignores Jane and moves in close to the girl. He is protected by a white marshmallow-looking jacket that seems too thick for the dreary yet humid night.

She tries to make eye contact with the girl, whose lids are fluttering. "Do you need some water?"

"She's with me," the man says. He's waiting for Jane to go. Jane prepares to scream if she has to. She can't remember the last time she made such a sound, a harsh echo from deep inside her throat. Maybe in her sleep.

"Leave her alone." Jane can see the glow of a hot dog stand from the other side of the alleyway and is comforted by the fact that other humans are close enough to hear her scream. The girl wobbles to her feet; the hem of her blue dress is up around her waist. She's wearing a pink thong. The man takes her arm and props it around his shoulders.

"Can I see your purse?" Jane asks the girl.

Jane moves between her and the man. It's easy to pull the girl's arm off his bulked shoulders as he is the same height as Jane. She takes the purse from the cold ground. Jane tries to keep a safe distance from the man but he moves around her.

"She's my girlfriend." He tries to smile as he says this. The girl's arm slips off Jane's shoulder and it takes Jane a moment to regain her balance.

"What's her name?" Jane thumbs through the clasped purse, feeling for cards: a driver's license, student card, and a credit card. The license says that she was born only a few years later than Jane—she's twenty. Jane glances at the restless man then at the girl, who has curled back into fetal position. The driver's license reads *Ramona Gregs*.

"What's your girlfriend's name?"

"Sassy cunt."

She could only ever run in sprints. Moments of racing through twilight bring her back to the pleased exuberance of being a child. She's been ready to run since this man showed up but wonders how fast she can go now that her central nervous system is so fucked.

She catches up to a group of people when she reaches the end of the alley. She waves frantically to get their attention, while looking back to see that the man has Ramona in his arms like he's a firefighter retrieving her from a smoking building. When he notices Jane waving to the group, he all but drops her and flees.

An ambulance is called for Ramona. Jane slips away before the group can really ask her anything. She's comfortable in the knowledge that Ramona Gregs is going to the nearest hospital.

She's unnerved enough to hail a cab she can't afford to get to Kitty's place. She's running low on the money she saved from the Fish Bar. She was supposed to be there half an hour ago but Kitty is used to Jane's tardiness. When Jane arrives she finds Kitty sitting on the floor propped up against her bed. She has her laptop open. Jane can hear the sounds of people fucking—probably Kitty and god knows who. Jane doesn't really feel like she has a part in their project anymore.

"I think I helped someone tonight," she says.

"See?" Kitty says this as if she saves people all the time. She closes the laptop and smiles up at Jane. "It doesn't take much time out of your day to help the world. That's beautiful."

Jane is put off by her friend's change, not knowing if altruism is a trait she has always carried that Jane has never noticed.

"So, it will be an installation?"

Kitty exhales and takes a moment to sip wine from a mason jar beside her—then she hands it to Jane. "I want there to be a sparkling light show that makes it look like you're in outer space. Then, I include the audio. One clip will start, playing from a hidden speaker on one side of the room. Three minutes later, another clip will play on the opposite side of the room. The last speaker will be installed in the ceiling and will start to play ten minutes into the show."

"Do we have money for this?" Jane takes a big gulp of the wine.

"They'll give us some money." Kitty waves her hand, refusing to take the glass back.

Jane can finish the rest. She is relieved that she has been working on her own thing. The band-aid painting.

Richard wants to meet to talk about the meaningless love affairs he has endured since they broke up. When they first sit down there is a calm silence between them. Jane occupies herself with a bowl of sugar cubes. She crumbles two all over the table then drops three more into her coffee. Coffee makes her shake. Everything makes her shake.

The café turns into a bar at night. Now that it gets dark earlier, the dimmed lights allow for the taxidermy animal decorations to be illuminated in a subtly demanding way. There is a fake-looking Arctic fox above Richard's head. He appears healthier than he did during the summer. Maybe he's run out of money for coke. His eyes are brighter and wider, though she'd mostly only seen him in bed.

"I think I maybe saved someone a few weeks ago."

"From what?"

"A bear." She says this with a deadpan stare.

"Clever."

"No, she was passed out in an alley."

"Wow, that sucks."

"Some dude tried to put her in his car."

"That could happen to you."

"No. I've really calmed down."

Richard was flippant with her while they were dating, making her feel taken yet alone. His sudden concern for her well-being strikes her as odd. She hates it when anyone comments on her habits. She needs time to decide what to do with him. She wants him to think she's laid off the booze by playing the angle of "the phase."

"So, things didn't pan out?" she asks, referring to a woman he'd mentioned a month earlier in one of the text messages she ignored.

"The sex was boring."

"Why?"

"It was just boring."

"Do you think we'll ever fuck again?"

"Don't ask that."

Richard gets up and Jane can see him paying the bill at the counter.

The last time Jane visited Anna she made a joke about zoning out during sex. Anna was concerned.

"Be mindful of your thoughts next time you transcend yourself," she said.

"Transcend myself?"

The only time Jane is enthusiastic about anything is when she's drunk. It's much too embarrassing to be into something while sober. It's like when she used to wear colours. She made some poor fashion choices during the time she wore colours and has regretted them ever since. Jane needs to appear complex and she believes that buying black clothing makes her so.

She looks at the speck on the pillow next to her as she pants, and she knows that Richard will turn her over in approximately forty-five seconds. She will act thrilled. She can't remember when she started dissociating.

So, there's the pillow. He's groaning. Maybe she zoned out before the pillow. He went down on her and did it too hard and she'd been embarrassed for him.

Maybe she dissociated before the sex started. Maybe it was when they were play-fighting and he won and hit her head against the peeling leather sofa. She said it was okay when he asked if it was too much. Maybe she thought their play-fighting was simply too intimate, like when someone you don't care about tells you a vital secret that could ruin them.

Jane has nothing to report to Anna the psychic saint who asks her to journal about her feelings. Anna always has magnificent coats. Maybe Jane can make a comment about that.

Today she's wearing a long leather jacket with a large black scarf. The jacket drips onto the toes of her thigh-high boots as they walk through the park. Not many people are out today. There are a few couples walking dogs. Some groups of people smoking pot together. Jane is beginning to think about the nuances of her relationship patterns, as well as her fascination with anything that will alter her mood.

Jane feels like she needs to learn from Anna at a more accelerated pace. At the very least from her fashion. Jane finds it interesting that she dresses differently during the day than she does at her place of work. Maybe everyone does that. Anna walks with a subtle confidence, her hands placed lightly inside the pockets of her leather coat, which Jane wouldn't have thought was Anna's style but now seems like a natural choice for her.

"Richard and I went for a coffee. I told him how I saved that person in the alley."

"When you talk about Richard, it reminds me . . ."

Jane is aware that Anna is about to launch into a story about her memories. It's okay. She likes the attention from someone older. Anyone older, it seems. Jane might be Anna's cheerleader. A younger soul who feeds Anna's confidence with her presence and confusion, as well as her ability to fail.

"Of what?" Jane is also becoming desperate to understand her circumstances. Her pain feels original in its dismantling of her logic.

Anna stops walking. She pulls one of her hands out of the coat, motioning for them to veer off the pathway towards a large maple tree. Then she pulls Jane close to her. Jane isn't sure what to do. Anna places her hands under Jane's elbows so they are left in a half-embrace. Her gaze steadies but it doesn't seem like she is really looking at Jane. It's an expression Jane hasn't seen from her—a look of hesitant wonder as if she has found something after a long search but is skeptical about it being real.

"I dated an old poet. I loved him very much."

Her words come out languid and weary, insinuating that Jane is supposed to know what dating an old poet means or is like.

"Okay." Jane has never had any interest in the poets she's met apart from Richard, who she doubts is a real one. They all seem a bit fucked.

"I loved him very much." Anna repeats these words not to Jane but to herself, with the puzzled look of someone who is trying to remember the name of an actor or solve a math problem with a technique they learned in grade school and forgot.

Anna continues, "He claimed that everyone wanted something from him, but I never did. He was just a hot guy who drank. I bossed him around a lot. I told him he was an idiot. People are just people, Jane."

"But you remember this person—why?"

"I believe he loved me too."

The seriousness of her tone moves Jane. It's like a prayer Anna has memorized for herself, one she banks on every day. It doesn't matter if it is real.

"I only cared about him because he was beautiful, and he took care of me when I would drink too much. We'd hook up all over the city, in the bathrooms of museums, in clubs, once inside a carousel that had been closed down for the night. I wanted him to take me home to meet his parents."

Jane doesn't feel the impulse to speak.

"I was about twenty years younger than him when we met. I thought he was my age. When I got to know him, I found that he had much more energy than I did. He'd always be up in the morning with some idea to rearrange his furniture, stuff like that. I decided that I wanted to work hard.

"I expected everything I did to be perfect. I used cocaine to help me work hard. The work I was aiming for was impossible, though, because it didn't exist. There is a difference between hard work and hurting yourself in the name of perfection. This pursuit usually means that you are trying to cover something up. Nothing is worth that kind of exertion. If you think something is, you should do it. Little things about my personality began to change. I started to like the same colours, people, clothes, and music that he liked. I didn't notice it. I was still learning how to be in the world."

As Anna releases Jane from their embrace, Jane notices that her hands feel quite dry. She wonders if hands are a preview of how the face will age. Anna's hands look bony and old, with creases that form a mosaic to the tips of her black-manicured fingers. Jane can't tell if she's doing this involuntarily, but she notices Anna start to do up her jacket, clasping each button and feeling it afterward as if she's checking that it's closed.

She waits for Anna to continue but it seems like she's done. Her leather coat is buckled high now and there is a large bulge near her neck from her thick scarf. The coat is covering her mouth but in a flattering way that is making her cheekbones look more pronounced.

"Was it fun, dating the poet?"

"Eventually I had to move into a basement apartment by myself. Before that I was at my parents'. They had to bring me food in bed because I couldn't move or eat. My depression was that bad. When I had enough strength to leave my parents' and move into the apartment, the first thing I did was find a little chest that I thought looked like the one in the place he and I had lived in. I put a silver gothic tea set on top, then some big books that I didn't like under each leg of the chest because it was sort of wobbly and I also wanted it to look taller. The chest is a dark burgundy. I still have it. He told me he wished that he could pull it all out of me, the darkness. I consider the burgundy chest to be a memorial, or a tribute to who I was during that time."

Therapists like Anna are just people, Jane thinks. Old poets are just people.

"The leaves are so crunchy." Jane touches Anna's arm in an effort to bring them both back to their current surroundings. She wants to tell Anna about a song she likes. It seems like a bad time to ask Anna if she feels obligated to go on this walk because Jane saved her child as a kid. Or maybe it's a good time. Jane can add her own dark confession of insecurity to the walk.

"They look like metallic death." Anna's steps grow faster. She continues, "I have dreams of seeing him again where we look at each other for three long minutes. Sometimes, when I'll accidently see a photo of him on the internet, I feel sick. I think he gave me celiac."

"You have celiac?"

"I did, but then it went away."

"Can it go away?"

"You can't let someone like that be so significant in your life, Jane. It doesn't have to be like that. You have to add meaning yourself. You have to find hope and purpose even when you're hungover by yourself—staring at the uneven paint job on the wall across from your bed."

She appreciates the way that Anna told the story—with an absence of self-pity that shows through her analysis of the bad experience and the way it changed her relationally. Maybe denial and self-pity can be both liberating and detrimental. The minute that self-pity is brought up it can be nurtured; it could be a rejection of agency over an event or feeling. Jane doesn't know how to express these thoughts to Anna.

"Thanks for sharing that with me."

"Once I wrote an essay that got a lot of praise. When I told some of my close friends, they were surprised."

"What was the essay about?"

"I was hoping that I would get a phone call from my former lover to congratulate me. This hope was a delusion. He would never read it."

"I asked you what the essay was about."

"I'm not sure I remember."

Jane doesn't push for the parts of the story that Anna isn't sharing. Acknowledging a trauma can lead to a slow deconstruction of a life, a reflection on choices that might not have been made by the affected person at all. Tastes in music, paintings, movies, everything is influenced by it. A personality most of all. Jane would rather take drugs than think about whatever sadness Anna is sharing. It is the true darkness, Jane knows this. A darkness that can't be described but is always there.

"It doesn't matter now. No one cares." Anna smiles thinly, not with her teeth but with her lips.

"I have to go work on some stuff for school."

Anna nods and gives her a hug that lasts longer than expected. Jane begins to walk away, feeling puzzled and drained. She wonders what it would be like to be more present—to feel what she is on the verge of feeling, all the time. A feeling she knows will be bad. She looks back at Anna, whose face is now in her hands.

Jane is sure she looks vacant and chill while she's being fucked—and if her detachment shows in a bad way, no one has ever called that out. She and Richard film themselves sometimes on Jane's cell phone. She only wants the videos on her phone because she worries that Richard will show Scotty, or someone else they know. She sort of wants him to. Richard always wants to watch and jerk off beside Jane. She'll replay the videos when she's bored or anxious, as if this disgusting fucking is an anchor to a desired neutral emotional state. She could ask Richard if she can add their sound effects to the art project. She probably won't.

While fucking, Jane doesn't know if her face is sleepy, sexy, or if she just looks like she's in pain.

"You're beyond words. You're gorgeous. Fuck," Richard will often say while they have sex—or that's something Jane imagines hearing as he grabs her ass and bites on her earlobe. It's as if he's panting the words out through strenuous exercise, or like he's about to die by his own hand. Maybe he really can't believe he's lying next to her. Jane is silent and tired.

"Try not to toss around tonight. I have a big day tomorrow." Richard kisses her freckled shoulder.

seven

Jane almost feels jealous because she's never had sex with anyone in a bathroom stall. She smirks when she meets the gaze of the man she's with. Kitty's being cool without knowing it. Jane hates this place. He appears amused. He'll laugh about this with his friends later if he remembers.

On the way into the club there were glass cases with mannequin heads inside of them dressed in colourful wigs and with eyelashes drawn on. They walked through a gauntlet of plastic heads, stopping to take pictures near the cases with the best wigs—sparkling silver and bright pink ones. They should have started the night pretending that they were different people by wearing more makeup, donning wigs like the mannequins, and choosing clothing that wasn't all black.

The bathroom smells like a gingerbread-scented candle and it is giving Jane a headache. Jane hasn't been wearing deodorant lately because she's developed a taste for her own musk. Jane's companion is made more attractive by his ennui and his height. His feigned boredom could be a defense mechanism. Jane likes the way she has to tilt her head sideways to make eye contact with him. He's wearing a black dress shirt with tight black jeans. They match.

He pulls out a baggie.

"You're going to get us kicked out."

He shrugs. "Then we'll go somewhere else."

"If anyone comes, I'll put it all inside my vagina."

"Whatever works!"

Jane pulls hand sanitizer from her bag so she can sterilize part of the counter. She instructs him to cut lines on the sanitized part but she's also worried that the alcoholic gel will make the coke dissolve. Jane's neurosis knows no bounds. He does two lines through a ten-dollar bill, which Jane thinks is a bit rude. He should have let her go first.

Jane yells Kitty's name, laughing as her friend exits the stall. Kitty wears the bemused half-smile she gets when she's fucked up. A man emerges expressionless, like he's concentrated on a lie he's about to tell someone.

The man from the stall is not as tall as the man Jane is with. He has bulky arms fit into a black button-up shirt. His blonde hair and pale skin make him look like he could be

Jane's brother. Jane checks to see that the coke has been cleared up and the four of them head out of the bathroom into the party.

Jane needs something urgently but she doesn't know what. Her stimulated, neurotic brain is telling her that she should be fucking her companion, in the same stall that Kitty was in, because that is what a true friend would do. She needs this man to become completely infatuated with her and she needs more cocaine and she needs to dance.

Jane bought coke off a man on the street a week ago during the horrible, constant drug pursuit that starts once she has some drinks. She tried to hide it from her friend until a night later Kitty was over and walked in on her in the bathroom. Kitty put her finger in the white powder and proclaimed that Jane couldn't even score proper coke. Jane bought the coke because she was worried about lasting at these ridiculous parties. Kitty has more stamina than she does. Stimulants allow Jane to drink for longer periods of time.

Kitty never would have fucked anyone here if they wanted to return. They hate this place but came because Kitty knows the DJ who is playing. The music is quite good. Dark, and without words.

"That was great," Kitty whispers.

"We heard." Jane laughs as they linger at the side of the dance floor. The man Kitty was with has gone to get more drinks. The tall man stares at his phone screen.

"You were listening?" Kitty won't remember this conversation.

Jane brushes her fingers through her already matted, sticky hair. Yes—that's why they're here. Bubbles. It's a foam party. A filthy foam party where some machine attached to the ceiling sprays bubbles and foam starting at midnight.

"Never." Jane feels for her phone in her pocket and wishes she had put it in a Ziploc bag to protect it from the wetness. What if someone breaks a bottle amidst the bubbles? She's happy she's wearing combat boots and that Kitty is wearing the same. She watches Kitty head to the centre of the dance floor where the bubbles pour from the ceiling.

After an hour, Jane's body is wet and her mind euphoric.

"What's your name again?" she asks the tall man while they dance.

"Sophocles."

"I don't believe you."

It would be funny if he was giving her a fake name. By now, the foam has accumulated into a grotesque blob in the middle of the dance floor. It spreads as the mist from a fog machine would and it has long since reached their feet. The room they're in is about the size of a gymnasium. There are other rooms. Sophocles stops dancing and pulls one of those pouches that look like half a wallet out of his front pocket. He looks like he's adjusting his dick in his pants. The wallet is dark brown leather.

He rifles through until he finds his ID and Jane finds it endearing that he seems to be in a rush to hand it to her.

Someone elbows her in the back. Sophocles doesn't catch her as she falls to the floor.

"Are you okay?" He helps her up. She's dropped his license. It's not a conversation she's ready to have with him. Her euphoria is fleeting and must be nurtured. It's telling her she needs to be in four places at once. She needs to do laps. To roll in the foam. She might even need to eat. If she closes her eyes, the music makes her feel like fucking.

"You have my ID?"

She kisses Sophocles and says, "No, let me make it up to you."

Next to them, Kitty is making out with this guy she's with. Jane wants them to finish so they can leave, and she almost wants to risk Kitty's anger by breaking the two of them up. Jane likes being fucked up enough to make plans for an entire group because it makes her feel like she can control the passage of time.

"But seriously, where is it?" Sophocles shouts in her ear. He's still smiling, though.

"I can't find it." She bends down and sticks her hand into the foam and feels the sharp end of something, perhaps a broken beer bottle. She needs to check if her hand is bleeding. Jane can't hear it but she can see Sophocles cursing. "Do you still find me attractive?" Jane shouts.

"What?"

"I'm kidding. You want to come to Kitty's house?"

"Is that your friend?" He points to Kitty and she's surprised he doesn't remember what just happened in the bathroom.

Kitty lives above a serious coffee shop that used to be a bank. Her studio loft is much more comfortable than Jane's basement. During the obligatory tour of the apartment, Kitty's guy pretends to look at a previous painting of hers—for too long—and makes some inane comment on the texture and the colours. Jane is worried about the liquor they have lasting, well, forever, or at least through to the morning. Sophocles says nothing about the painting and Jane respects him for this. Sophocles motions for them to sit on the floor around a low coffee table made of oak. It looks very expensive. The guy Kitty is with claims that sitting on the floor is an equalizer.

Sophocles has large eyes with thick lashes that make everything he says seem like the truth.

In Jane's paranoid mind, their conversation is being recorded on someone's phone. *Watch what you say, idiot. Be kind to yourself. You're okay. Sophocles is going to love you. Why do you care?* It's thoughts like these that often lead to her overdoing it, taking more of whatever's around to make her interior narrative disappear. She's at the stage where she knows she needs more; the tricky line she walks every time she makes promises to herself about only drinking beer. It's when she becomes quiet and the men she sees ask her why she won't speak. She doesn't trust anyone during these internal digressions. Sophocles rubs her thigh and she knows if she takes a bit more of anything, she'll be a decent human.

Jane goes through the mental checklist she has when coke is around: Will there be enough? How sad will I be when it's gone? Is there alcohol for when it's over? Is there pot?

There's pot, for later, and the emergency whiskey hidden in her laundry hamper for when she gets home. The bottle she keeps in case all the stores are closed and she is withdrawing. In case there's an unforeseen bank holiday. Repulsion and attraction to liquor are starting to look the same but that's not something she wants to worry about tonight. She takes one of Kitty's books with the intention of using it for the coke, noting that there are an odd number of pages in the book. She feels comfortable with odd numbers. While handing the book to the guy Kitty brought, Jane notices that she has lit candles around the room, which sort of smells like feet. There are shoes and clothes in odd places. One red heel wedged in the couch with a cigarette burn on it. An excellent fall coat hanging on a nail next to a painting of a flamingo. Jane is relieved that the curtains are closed. The guy with the coke wipes the book with the bottom of his shirt before he pours half the bag onto it.

"What's your name again?" Jane knows that Kitty's guy has told her at least four times tonight, and for the first time he looks annoyed.

"August Brown."

"That sounds like a fake name," Kitty says in a high-pitched voice that comes out when she's a bit fucked. "I want a fake name."

"It seems like everyone already has a pseudonym." Jane tries to wink at Sophocles but he gives her the confused bashful smile of someone who is turned on and doesn't know why. August takes the first line. After he's done he says, "Everything is more fun with fake names."

"I'll be Jane Craig." Jane Berkeley has always hated the abrasiveness of her own name. She also doesn't possess enough creativity to think of an entirely new name. It's too much pressure, like trying to think of something to post on Twitter, or a caption for a photo online.

"Didn't you tell me your name is Jane already? Or has that been your fake name all along?" The man known as August looks confused. Jane realizes that he doesn't know her last name, so the subtle change she's made is lost on him.

"I'll be Katerina Karenina," Kitty says.

"Why not just make it Anna?" asks Sophocles and Jane likes him for knowing what book it's from.

"Anna Karenina." Kitty is proud to have made the connection and Jane is proud for her.

"Let's add this," August says, as he pulls out another baggie.

"This isn't ketamine, is it?" Jane asks as a joke, but it isn't really a joke.

"Do you know what ketamine is?" August is smiling with his eyebrows raised. It is the look of someone who is about to win a game of chess, or of someone who has confused their enemy. August is not Jane's enemy yet.

"Forgive me, for I am simple." She blinks her eyes, then lowers them and gives him a smile as though she has made a mistake and knows about it. Then she adds, "You can mix them."

"That's what we're planning on doing." August smiles. "If that's okay with you?"

"It's cool," Kitty says.

August pours some of the contents of the new baggie onto the coke that is on top of the book. He traces out four new lines. Jane recalls the only time she took ketamine.

The Time I Took Ketamine by Mistake by Jane Berkeley

The time I took ketamine by mistake was not my fault. My therapist has reassured me. I thought it was coke. When I accidentally took ketamine, I saw balloons and abrasive strobe-lights that turned into neon spirals. I felt more drunk than usual. The silver balloons near the bar started to look like stretched-out playdough. I tried to find purpose in every step that I took to the washroom, but I fell on someone's table and their drinks spilled. It was clear I couldn't handle ketamine. After that, people who I thought were friends sent me messages telling me I was out of control. It was unnecessary. I am not sorry for taking ketamine by mistake, but I wish I had done it in a cooler place with better people.

The book they're using of Kitty's is about psychic voyages. It's black with a holographic human figure on the cover. Each chapter examines a different theory from the psychic world and how it occurs. Come to think of it, Anna must have a copy. The lines are pretty thick, and they circle each corner of the square image of the figure on the book. Jane likes that August did that.

"Who wants to go?" he asks.

"Me," Jane says.

There are a total of three diary entries in the leather notebook Jane received for her birthday from Richard. The ketamine entry is important to her, reminding her how weird things can get. She has it memorized and recites it to herself when she's in situations where there is little light and everyone around her is high. She usually does whatever is around her anyway. Reciting the entry still comforts her. She tried.

Kitty has decided to play a melodramatic film score that is simple and repetitive on her phone, which is connected to a couple of large speakers Jane knows she got for her birthday from her older brother. The rising splendour of the string music makes Jane's thought process seem pathetic, like she is so easily entertained by a film score made to entertain millions. Kitty lights a cigarette with one of the candles and almost burns her eyelashes.

"Be fucking careful," Jane shouts, knowing that Kitty is fucked but also is scared of fire.

There is a sullen silence. Her outburst seems to have broken the joyful recklessness of the evening.

"Do you think our lives are so boring that we have to listen to inspirational movie soundtracks?" Sophocles asks, interrupting the silence.

"Do any of you listen to whale sounds?" August is grinding his teeth visibly.

"No, but I will now." Jane's shoulders tighten. She'd be scared if she were in an ocean in front of a blue whale. Photographs of divers with their underwater cameras right in front of the whale's big mouth flash into her mind. If it were Jane, she would be frightened that the whale would swallow her forever. She's not frightened by death but of having to live trapped, knowing she was going to die slowly.

Kitty walks back to her phone. She takes a bit of time to zone out and have a scroll before she raises her eyes to the room.

"Let's start with ocean waves."

The ocean waves sound nice to Jane at first. Then they all start to blur into a sound she recognizes.

"The ocean waves just sound like an oscillating fan."

"Jane, why the fuck are you ruining the ocean waves?"

"Maybe we can try like, a different recording?"

"What did the waves do to you?" Kitty feigns anger which is something Jane knows she does when she is irritated and wants to hide it.

"I want to hear the whales," Jane says blandly.

"The band?" Sophocles chimes in.

"There's a band called the Whales?" Kitty asks.

"Probably, but I just made that up."

Kitty walks back to her phone with an extra pounce in her step that Jane chooses to note as her determination to please the room. She puts on an ambient mix that Jane showed her a couple of days ago.

"I think music helps us interpret certain emotions." August's words come out fast.

Jane is starting to like August more than Sophocles, possibly because she's having difficulty differentiating between the two at this point.

"But how can you interpret an emotion you can't name?" Sophocles says and Jane knows she can gain something from him. Some knowledge. A clue. These conversations about nothing are beginning to bore her. Jane wants things with these strangers to get messy, faster, so she can watch other people feel intensity.

"What do you mean?" Kitty says as she pulls her hair into a bun on the top of her head.

"No word in the English language can encompass the feelings we get from music," Jane says, knowing she sounds profound, quickly moving from her introspective stage to an extroversion, which could embarrass her.

"Music tends to evoke primary emotions." Sophocles talks like he's speaking to a group of students—which he is, essentially, and for the first time she notices that he must be at least ten years older than the other three.

"Is the song a primary emotion?" Kitty says, as if she has had a gradual realization.

"What does it make you feel?" August smiles and levels his eyes in a way that looks both calm and condescending.

"Love would be a primary emotion and affection a secondary emotion," Jane says, not knowing if that's right at all.

"I mean, sometimes with the music it's the sickness you feel in your stomach and it's the fact that you want to cry and throw up but you can't do those things any longer. It can hit you, hard, but only for a minute, then you're back to feeling neutral and the cello almost taught you what life is worth living for." There is a pause after Kitty makes this statement. The men look at each other.

"I have an idea," says Jane as she motions for the book

with the coke and ketamine. She doesn't like Kitty sounding eloquent when they're all fucked up. "Let's play Exquisite Corpse and write down what the cello makes us think of."

"That's a fucking dumb idea." Kitty laughs. She sounds embarrassed.

"Sure," August says.

"I don't have any paper," Kitty says.

They quickly forget about Exquisite Corpse.

Jane doesn't know how to verbalize that she wants more drugs. She's been holding on to the feeling of elation like it's her last hope but she can barely recognize it anymore. Euphoria and the anxiety of it ending have merged into something Jane can no longer understand or control. Kitty seems calm and confident. Jane is depressed by the knowledge that she is the only person in the room with such a debilitating thought process. The rest of them know how to have fun.

While the others surround a bar cart of Kitty's that's piled with liquor and bitters, Jane takes what she thinks is the coke baggie into the bathroom and pours half of it inside her locket necklace. It could be the ketamine but mostly smells like coke. She sets an alarm on her phone to remind herself that she has to be careful with the necklace. There's valuable shit inside of it. She looks at the time on her phone and tells herself that if the current time ends in an odd number her friends will notice what she's done and if it's an even number, they'll think they did the coke themselves. She takes a photo of her face in the mirror and posts it on social media then deletes it because it's two in the morning and her eyes look sad.

There is a man who uses the swing set in the park beside Jane's window at night. Jane met him once when she was standing on a corner having a cigarette before going to Kitty's, holding a bag full of speakers that she'd found at Value Village to be used in their project. Her worries that he would jump off the swing when it was mid-air were assuaged when he went for it and landed softly on his feet. He strolled over to her and asked if he could have a cigarette. She said yes. He introduced himself as Samuel but the interaction unnerved Jane because he appeared manic—even after his calm exit from the swing.

She can often trace his silhouette as she paints. Through her basement window he's swinging with giant headphones bobbing as he pumps higher and higher. He often does this late at night.

The ringer on Jane's phone seems purposefully abrasive. In the phone's settings, it's titled "Whimsical Dream." She can't pinpoint exactly what nuanced trauma she projects onto the darting sound of her phone's trilling bells, or its title. The tone is also a release, prompting Jane to drop whatever she is doing and lie in her bed, where she will try to ask whoever is calling about their day. She's trying to talk about herself less. Kitty is the only one who calls this late. She's found someone who will provide even more speakers for their supposed collaboration.

After hanging up, Jane gets out of bed and looks at internet photos of Dorothea Tanning, Lucian Freud, and Egon Schiele paintings while opening tabs she's pinned with techno mixes. She remembers Anna telling her that she must create the basics before anything else. She hopes Kitty doesn't find out that she is entering the competition alone. It's not like Jane will win. Whenever Kitty comes over, she hides the painting in the laundry hamper, the same place she stores her emergency whiskey, careful to gently stroke the paint to make sure it's dry before she places a white bedsheet over it.

The techno sounds wrong. Jane walks over to her computer to investigate and is embarrassed when she finds that two mixes in separate windows are playing at the same time. At least she noticed, eventually. She pauses them both. Now she's able to hear the familiar creak of the rusty chains that signals Samuel's compulsive swinging. The sound is mixed with the cackle of bubbles popping inside a can of soda water that's next to her computer. She moves the can because she's worried she'll spill it on the laptop. Jane is trying not to drink so she's switched to beer and wine only, and before she starts with that, she drinks soda water for as long as she can.

She imagines the conversation she and Samuel would have if she were to go have a smoke with him, or even worse, invite him in. She drinks and fucks. Paints, sometimes. He swings. She sometimes notices him at the coffee shop nearby, the way a person notices someone who is staring at them. She wonders why he feels she can help him, why he wants to be her friend. Jane has Kitty, Anna, and sometimes Richard, so it's possible that she's set for emotional support.

But really she's tired and lonely. The band-aids and dark circles are still under her new coats of paint, her new attempts to find a certain subtlety that will contrast with the chaos of her life. She wants sex. She wants the painting to be done. She wants to go to another country to find happiness.

She looks at the photograph she's copying, one that Richard took when they were fucked on pills, and wonders why she can't emulate the murky sludge of the water she's in. How a shade can emulate a feeling. Red. Yellow. Blue. Happiness. Anger. Hurt. Sadness. She remembers being in grade school—very young—and deciding to dip the brush in every colour and flick her wrist to spray the canvas with little dots of paint. The voice of her teacher sounds muffled and submerged like the adults in Charlie Brown cartoons and only becomes recognizable in its extreme annoyance and disappointment. "What have you done?" She'd sprayed paint all over the room, even managing to cover the kid next to her.

Now the water in the painting is grey. It looks filthy. The swings continue to creak ominously, reminding Jane of the last vivid dream she had and how she felt like it was about loneliness, if you can dream about that.

eight

Kitty paces her apartment with the subdued energy of someone who's experiencing a gradual realization. "I can't believe we lost."

Jane wants to say, "I can." But instead she continues to watch Kitty walk slowly, pulling at her hair strand by strand. She hasn't noticed this habit of hers.

Two days ago, Jane received an e-mail awarding her the travel scholarship. She's spent the last forty-eight hours thinking of how to tell Kitty.

"I wonder who won."

"Kitty, I did."

"You entered your own piece too?"

"Yes, so we'd have more of a chance."

"You're going to split the money with me?"

It's an option. Going to London by herself wouldn't be much fun and she'd end up on FaceTime with Kitty. It seems like a pretty good amount of money but she doesn't really want to divide it in half. Her living arrangements are paid for as well as her flight. There's spending cash.

"I have my own money. I'll tag along."

"You're not mad, are you?"

"Entering alone was part of your journey." She walks over to the couch and flips onto her back, leaving her legs dangling off. There is something about Kitty that always leaves Jane on the edge of truly trusting her, and Jane wonders if Kitty ever cared about the contest or their collaboration. It has to do with the fact that she agrees to pretty much everything. It's not that she's always down to do drugs. That's fine. It's these projects she takes on, especially theirs, that make Jane wonder if she even wants to work, or if she just wants to appear to be a person who is *doing a lot*. Jane doesn't know if it's jealousy of the way Kitty manages things or the way she manages people. She wanted there to be something pure about the thing that they were doing together, and for a sense of commitment and loyalty to be reciprocated.

"What money do you have?"

"Don't worry about it." Kitty's voice sounds rushed and foreign. Then she goes silent, her eyes squinting at the ceiling above her as if she is counting the number of marks in the pattern or solving a mathematical problem in her head. "Enough." She breaks from her gloom, sitting up. "I've been wanting to take a trip for a while!"

"I'm excited."

"What did you submit in the end?"

"This." Jane takes a moment to rifle through the 2,750 photos on her phone, most of which are of her face. She flashes a photograph of the painting, watching the light from the phone reflect on Kitty's nose.

"That is a good piece," Kitty says calmly, in a way that reassures Jane mostly because Kitty wouldn't say anything at all if it was bad.

"You don't think I'm desperate?" Jane says, then quickly regrets it.

"For what? No, not like some people we know."

"Who?"

"The careerists, like, what do they do if they fail? What do they do if something happens that makes them unable to do their art anymore?" Kitty says.

"Yeah, exactly." Jane doesn't want Kitty to know at this point that she is one of these people. Not someone who will step on another to get ahead, just someone who cannot fail. The unsettling image of her own drinking comes to mind when Kitty mentions the prospect of something making a person unable to do their art.

"Failing is fine," Jane adds. "But not being able to do it anymore would suck."

"Some of these people. You know? It's just nonsense."

"People really need to chill."

"Yeah."

"I just want to do my stuff. I don't really care what happens with it," Jane lies. "Maybe someone will find it when I die." She says this with the knowledge that it is the correct remark in a situation where one can easily be accused of not caring about their art but about recognition. Jane doesn't know what she wants in terms of recognition, but she knows she wants something.

"But it's okay to want a career," Kitty ruminates, and this makes Jane feel powerful. The lies she tells Kitty show that Jane is more aware of the situation as well as different opinions regarding the situation of wanting a career. In contrast, Kitty is still figuring it out, thinking out loud, and it is this specific vulnerability of Kitty's that Jane strives to live without.

"Yeah, for sure."

"But not too much." Kitty lights a cigarette, which is unusual because she is vocal about how much she hates the smell of cigarettes indoors.

"You're good, otherwise I wouldn't be your friend." Kitty pauses, flipping through her phone. She pulls up a Facebook profile of a man with ginger in his stubble. He looks about forty. "Do you find this man attractive?"

"He's okay." Jane is no longer comforted by the fact that Kitty said her piece is good. She could be lying. She could make fun of it with someone else later. But maybe it doesn't matter what Kitty thinks anymore. Jane won.

"He seems like a good fuck." Kitty is eating pecans from a resealable green bag she usually keeps by her bed for when she's hungover. Neither of them really has much of an appetite after all the drugs.

"Do you ever just zone out?"

"In a good way."

"In the best way," Jane agrees, lighting a smoke since Kitty has already signalled that it's okay. She makes a show of ashing it into one of the empty cups that held their Americanos a few mornings ago. It's sort of gross that the cups are still there, near her bed. Jane knows she personally doesn't zone out in a good way—she does so too often and with great sadness. She thinks of the bottle of Canadian Club in her purse and wonders if it will put Kitty off if she pulls it out. It's two in the afternoon.

"Let's not smoke after these are done," Kitty says. "I already regret it."

"Okay, I'm sorry."

"I'm quitting both cigarettes and dating."

"Then why did you show me that man?" Jane asks as she

heads to the bathroom with her mini-backpack, wondering if Kitty knows that she's leaving to drink secretly. She decides to practice the positive self-talk Anna was telling her about the last time they spoke on the phone. But Jane has her own version of positive self-talk. *It's just your paranoia. Drink.* Kitty will never know because Jane is meticulous with her concealment.

When Jane is finished, she returns to find Kitty standing up. Jane hadn't noticed what she's wearing, tights and a long black t-shirt with a picture of a devil. There is a frenetic energy about her as she begins to sort items in her apartment: garbage, pot, powder drugs, empty bottles, colourful heels, and a tube of her coral lipstick that is missing a lid. She darts around, putting her things into piles.

"What did you write in your application that we didn't write in ours?" Kitty asks.

"That I need to see a special exhibit on Pre-Raphaelite women portraiture and take a workshop run by the curator."

"I wish I'd thought of something like that." Kitty pours boxed wine into a glass for Jane. She wouldn't be doing so if she suspected Jane was drinking in the bathroom. "But it doesn't make much sense. You've never been into that."

Jane knew that Kitty's temperance wouldn't last long, in terms of substance use and in her reaction. She doesn't know what Kitty cares about. Is it jealousy about her winning the grant? Does Kitty just want to be invited to London with Jane?

"You don't really paint portraits," Kitty says.

"There is a lot you don't know about me."

"I should have applied myself and asked to go to the Magritte Museum."

"Belgium? You'd get bored there after two days."

"Maybe, without you. There's beer."

"Do you really like Magritte?"

"I like his work enough. I'm bored here. I also could have picked something I wanted to see at the Tate Modern. Or maybe I'll just go to Berlin with my money."

"Yes, your money. Berlin?"

"Yeah, I've always wanted to go but don't know why."

"Could work."

"I'll come with you to London. It's expensive there, but we'll find some fun."

"At least one of us got the grant."

"I truly can't believe it." Kitty opens a recycling bag and starts to put bottles into it so that they clink together abrasively.

"Do you need help?" Jane offers.

"No."

The stairs to Anna's office are steeper than Jane remembers. She plants herself in a chair, listening to a man groan behind one of the curtains. After mindlessly skimming through twenty pages of the novel she's been carrying around for a month, Jane's left wondering if she can still read—if her drinking will let her do that. She pretends to read books to prove her drinking is not affecting her ability to retain information.

"Shhh. He's almost asleep." Anna appears beside Jane, chiding her even though Jane is quietly reading.

"How long is he staying?"

"Until he wakes up and pays more."

"I won the travel grant."

"I keep doing e-mail surveys. You know those ones they show you on a receipt when you're finished paying at the drug store? I never win."

"We're going to London."

"Who's we?"

"Kitty. She's coming."

"Why would you waste your money on her when you won?"

"She's my friend. I'd happily spend money on her. But it turns out she has her own."

"Okay. Have you filled out your drinking journal?"

"Yes." Jane pulls a crumpled piece of paper out of her bag. On it, there's a chart that tracks how many drinks Jane has per day and her mood when she drinks them. This time Jane lied in her drinking journal, after searching the internet for the proper amount for a woman to drink in a week.

Anna flattens the piece of paper and looks at it, frowning. She hands it back to Jane.

"I'm sorry." Jane feels like crying because she's paranoid that Anna knows she lied.

"Will you be okay in London?"

"Kitty will be there."

They hear a small thud and a man emerges from behind the curtain. There are grey and black hairs on his stomach, sticking out of the seersucker shirt that he's still buttoning up. Jane wonders what boredom led him here—if he took a photo of the decorations outside. Anna is alluring, with the lightness of someone who was once complimented on traits like tenacity and being mischievous. She's mentioned to Jane that men have told her she is a manipulative bitch. She laughs when she recounts that. Anna's detached attitude comes out sometimes, in her interactions with guests and sometimes even with Jane. She suspects that it comes from a place where something inside of her died, perhaps from the sublime—yet common—heartbreak that she mentioned on their walk. Still, Anna carries the calculated, hungry look of an apex predator. It is the look of someone who has dedicated their life to non-violent revenge, someone who has remodelled their brain to replay the calculated dream of it.

The man is not unattractive. His eyes seem to glow. They are curious and very blue, giving way to a beauty he perhaps thrived from in his youth, and introducing the possibility of a charm that was still there in a sad way. His stubble, too, is both grey and black. Anna smiles like she knows a secret then jolts, as if she's just realized she's still in the same room as Jane. Perhaps this man doesn't want to pay in front of another person, or he isn't paying at all.

Anna turns back to Jane. "What does Kitty have to offer? Will you get a chance to work with her over there?"

"Her devotion." Jane is making a joke that will not be taken as a joke by Anna.

"And what does her devotion mean? Is this someone you will still talk to in ten years?" The man approaches Anna and begins to massage her back. Her lips press together, and her eyebrows rise in a way that makes her look both bored and amused. It is then that Jane understands that Anna is having an experience with the man. She prepares to leave.

While gathering her scarf, mini-backpack, and the leather jacket that she is now wearing over an insulated vest during the late fall, Jane pulls her headphones from her bag and wonders if it's dangerous for her to walk home alone at night with repetitive electronic music blasting. Anna is watching the man pour bourbon for them both. Jane heads towards the door, looking back to make eye contact with this older woman, one she has come to know and need, to say goodbye.

Jane grasps Kitty's hand because she's scared of flying as well as of contained spaces. Kitty recoils when Jane touches her. There is an announcement about free Wi-Fi that calms Jane a bit. The e-mail she sends to Anna is direct, desperate, and could even be considered insightful if read by the right person: *What does being an alcoholic really mean?*

"Kitty, do you think we're running away from something?"

"Shut up."

Kitty's response makes Jane flinch. She turns her body away from Kitty, leaning her head on the tiny oval window. Jane feels like she is an irritating younger sibling who Kitty can't get rid of. Still, she wants to try and talk to her.

"Has anything bad ever happened to you?" Jane had imagined their time on the plane as a chance to establish further intimacy with her friend. Apparently by asking blunt, awkward questions. A couple nights ago Kitty said she wanted to get drunk and fall asleep on the plane.

"I told you what happened." Kitty signals to the man pushing the drink and snack cart, who's wearing slacks that go up to his nipples. Jane respects that. His nametag reads *Gerald*. He gives her a nod to signal that he's on his way. The voyage of the drink cart can take an eternity on a plane.

"Of course, I'm so sorry." Jane doesn't remember Kitty telling her anything disturbing from the past. Perhaps she witnessed some confession during a blackout.

Gerald approaches them with the snack cart and Kitty asks how much the cheese plate costs, then starts a conversation with the man who is seated next to them in the aisle seat about how she wants to become a flight attendant.

"I should learn French," she laughs.

"My dad wanted me to learn French."

"And did you?" Jane interjects. Kitty and the man both pause and look at Jane.

"*Un peu.* My parents had high expectations of me." Kitty smirks while she's speaking and Jane doesn't understand the joke.

"Had?"

While Kitty chats with the man about her future linguistic possibilities, Jane reaches over and grabs a cheese plate from the food buggy and stuffs it under Kitty's seat. Not getting noticed is an accomplishment, considering she's reached over everyone's lap. She grabbed the cheese then made a show of looking for something on the floor. If the attendant noticed, he doesn't show it when he pours their drinks. Kitty laughs as Gerald pushes the cart away.

"You're going to get us kicked off," Kitty whispers so the man next to them doesn't hear. She sips her drink. Jane downs hers fast in order to trick her brain and prolong the experience of euphoria she got from stealing. Her stomach feels warm.

"I need some quiet time," Kitty says as she pulls out her headphones, ones that Jane thought she'd lost. Maybe she bought new ones? Kitty is often showing up with surprising new, nice things. Kitty begins to poke at the touch screen on the back of the seat in front of her, selecting a romantic comedy.

"Why are you watching such stupid, generic, formulaic shit?"

"Life is long, and this is what I consider fun." The line sounds rehearsed, and Jane is sure she's heard it before.

"Kitty, just talk to me. I'm bored."

Kitty lets out a frustrated groan and takes out one of her headphones. "When I was younger, I got caught masturbating at daycare. I was just a kid and I didn't know what I was doing. This woman came up to me all rushed and panicked and told me never to do that."

"Whoa."

"So I don't really masturbate."

"You don't?"

"No, I just wait for someone to make me come."

"You should get a vibrator."

"Never had one."

Kitty hasn't travelled to London before. Jane wishes she'd been here as an adult, when she had some experience with drinking, so she would know cooler places to show her friend. She's only been to London once, as a child on a family vacation.

After getting off the plane, Jane feels disoriented and desperate for a cigarette. She and Kitty walk towards a sign for a shuttle into the city. There are too many different trains listed and Jane can't figure out which one will take them downtown. She begins to feel like the trip has already failed. She wants to cry.

Kitty sees Jane's body seize up and sighs, irritated. "I'll go ask them."

She walks over to a group of women who are stylishly dressed and look to be in their early thirties.

Since Kitty doesn't have an inferiority complex, her personality welcomes new friends. This natural confidence and her above-average prettiness allow people to gravitate towards her and feel comfortable. Jane knows she is often said to have a perverse sense of humour—*dark and dry* is the kind way of labelling her coping mechanism in life. This makes it harder for her to meet people, and it is for this reason Jane needs Kitty. The connector. She envies the ease with which Kitty chats and laughs with these women. One of them points to the sign that reads *Gatwick Express*.

They pass a cluster of brightly lit stores advertising cheap prices on perfume, liquor, makeup, and skincare products. Jane notices one that is selling lingerie. Jane motions for Kitty to go inside with her. Kitty sighs again and when Jane catches her doing that, Kitty smiles widely in a way that makes her tired face turn into a grimace.

Inside the store Jane asks, "Do you sell vibrators?"

"Over there," says the person working there, pointing to the back corner of the store. The vibrators are all on sale. There is a gold one that is marked down to seven pounds.

"I'm buying it for you," Jane says.

"I'll buy it myself."

"We'll both buy one."

"Okay."

"Will you use it?"

Kitty shrugs. "I just think it's kind of funny that we're buying vibrators at Gatwick."

"It's chill."

"No one cares."

"Let's tell everyone we know or put it in our bio."

"Let's go to sleep."

"Yeah, we need to go to the hotel," Jane says. "Is the room big, do you think, or will we be sleeping on top of each other on a single bed? You know how those London rooms are." Jane has no idea how they could be.

"What are you afraid of?"

"That our room will actually be a cupboard with the bed next to the toilet."

"You'll have to just sleep on the toilet, then."

On the train Jane looks at Kitty, who is falling asleep next to her. She wants to ask her how it is so easy. How do people, places, and things always come so easily to her? Why does everyone like her so much? Jane feels foolish staring at her friend on the train. Kitty is kind of awful sometimes. It's difficult to pinpoint how. In these situations—ones where she is close to being threatened or jealous—she tries to remind herself of the structural mechanisms that pit her against other women. There is room for both of them. It isn't always easy for her to remember that, and she hates herself for it.

In the hotel room, Jane makes her way to the large, sterile-looking bed in order to rest. The last thought she has before falling asleep is about what it would be like to be fucked here, mostly by Richard. More thoughts come about what Richard must be doing now, considering the time difference—mainly, who he might be fucking right now. He could have moved on, as she has no idea if they're broken up forever. It doesn't really matter. She'll dream of him, or someone else, in a minute.

On the first day of the workshop, Jane has to leave the Underground midway to phone Kitty for directions.

"It's Charing Cross, like I told you. Why don't you just ask someone?"

"I don't want anyone to know I'm a tourist."

"You will never see them again."

"Meet me after?"

"Yeah."

After a short ride, she reaches the gallery.

In the meeting room at the gallery where the workshop is being held, everyone seated around the large folding table turns out to be over fifty. This brings Jane great comfort. They study her with curiosity when she walks in. Jane is relieved she is wearing what she feels most comfortable in: a black t-shirt and high-waisted black jeans. She considered trying to dress up. She regrets wearing makeup.

"Are you lost?" the instructor asks.

"No. I'm right where I need to be," Jane says. Internally she feels like the question is an attack. She's late, and at least twenty-five years younger than everyone else. That could be why she was asked.

"We have just finished introducing ourselves and describing one goal we have for our practice. One thing we want to get out of our time here." There is no chair left for Jane. "We can't bring in another chair because of the fire code. But I'll sit on the floor, dear."

Jane doesn't want the instructor to sit on the floor. Not that she seems too weak to do such a thing. It's just something Jane would rather do for her. She has grey-white hair and wide eyes that make her look a bit mad in a good way.

"I'll sit. I like it on the floor."

"I don't want to put you on the spot, but can you tell us something about yourself?"

"I'm very grateful to be here. I'm from Toronto. I like to listen to techno music."

"That's nice, dear."

She wonders what she will get out of learning about the Pre-Raphaelite sisterhood and sketching, which she hasn't done in years. Every so often, school children tethered to a rope led by their teacher walk by the door and break her concentration. She understands it's used to keep the kids together, from getting lost. She wonders why none of the kids ever let go of the rope and run away.

A couple of hours pass while the opportune light fades. She's scribbled some notes in a miniature notebook she bought at a dollar store, one with a photo of a dolphin on it. She's written something about women with long hair and its figurative connection to fertility that could easily be found on the internet. She's drawn a bunch of circles and traced their interiors in a calculated way that she feels would correlate with the industrial techno she is not listening to. Does the music lead to anger, or absolute calm?

Jane avoids speaking to anyone, walking fast towards the overpriced gallery café to meet Kitty. Her friend has company. Not wanting to bother them right away, Jane shuffles her feet into a turn that could be interpreted as a dance, heading back into the gallery. Then she's making awkward eye contact with men who she perceives to be staring at her. She compares the faces of the men to the portraits on the walls. They are like ghosts, or maybe even like novels—stopgaps where people are frozen during a certain period of their life, forever. The intensity of this comparison, of her own reluctance, fear, or inaptitude to do the same makes her feel drowsy. She'll go back to the café for a coffee. Some caffeine could help.

"We're going to a show tonight. Justin here has invited us." Kitty places her hand on his arm.

"It will be a once-in-a-lifetime musical orgasm." Justin nods his head while he says this as if he's affirming a definite positive outcome. He is the kind of man who is just tall enough to brag about his height. He's wearing a navy blue suit jacket with leather pants. Jane wonders if his pants are real leather, if she will ever be able to afford leather pants, and whether or not it would be gauche to ask this man about them.

"Cool, what show?" Jane immediately regrets the eagerness of her voice.

Justin shrugs. "I forget the name of the artist." His eyes are flecked with blue and orange. Normally Jane would question the fact that he can't remember the name of the musician whose stylings are so good that they're going to make them all come. But maybe this new term—"musical orgasm"—isn't meant to be taken literally.

"Naturally. Musical orgasm."

"I'd better go." Justin stands up while he pulls on a pair of leather gloves.

"Bye, Justin."

"I'll let you know the address," he says, mostly to Kitty.

Kitty and Jane continue to sit in the sterile café. They nurse their drinks in silence while Jane wonders what brought Justin here in the first place. The gallery café isn't exactly cool.

"He has grey in his beard. Aren't I the one who usually goes for the oldies?" Jane wants to make fun of his appearance even though she considers him a truly beautiful man.

"He just came up to me. He seems like he'll have drugs."

"Fair. I don't want to pay for anything."

That night, Justin calls them with an exciting piece of information, which is not the address but the fact that there is a car waiting for them outside. When they burst out of the front door of the hotel, they stop to look around. Jane wonders if they're on the receiving end of a prank. They notice a black town car across the street and walk over to it. When the driver gets out of the front seat and opens the back door for them, their relief is palpable. They're good to move on to their own private acknowledgement of the strangeness of their situation. The luxury is hilarious—as well as so unexpected that they feel compelled to do whatever the bringer of such luxury says. Kitty and Jane could stop and think about how dangerous getting into the random car could be. They don't. It's hard to tell if such excess will come again. The driver brings them to a warehouse. "It's being turned into a block of flats. Enjoy," he says as he opens the door for them.

The party they go to is just like any other party, but it is better because it is happening in another country. Jane knows they could be doing this back home. They are just doing the same thing with the same men, who happen to have different accents.

These private cars and parties continue. Kitty is obsessed with Justin—claiming he is a genius with a gentle bedside manner. But it is easy to confuse someone for a genius when there are so many drugs around. Drugs that don't have names, drugs that are mistaken for other things. Jane doesn't care what she takes as long as she has enough booze hidden somewhere. Justin comes from a wealthy family. His parents live in the country, but he spends a lot of time in their London flat. Neither of the girls is sure of what he really does. He says he works as a rare book preservationist. He winks often— at everyone.

Jane used to read and make collages when she was younger. She liked to control what the pictures she cut from magazines meant; once she cut them up and placed them on top of each other they took on different shapes and signifiers. Her parents gave her a lot of books about history. She enjoyed learning about all the Greek myths, the Egyptian pyramids. There were many books about fairies. Her mother even gave her a biography of Leo DiCaprio at one point because they had watched the movie *Titanic* together and Jane had mentioned she liked him.

Jane was reading about the pyramids and got really scared one night when she learned that they locked people inside them while they were still alive as a sacrifice to the gods. She ran into the dining room where her parents were having dinner and told them that she was convinced she was going to be locked away forever—that someone was going to trick her into walking into a pyramid and leave her there. This fear felt very real to Jane. Her mother put down her fork and stood up to gather some dishes. Her father poured the scant remainder of the bottle of wine that was on the table into his glass and then gave it to Jane. He motioned for her to sit in the chair that her mother had just vacated.

"You have a rather active imagination, my dear."

"It was scary."

"Would you like to try some wine? You'll be having it with us at dinner in a few years."

Jane thought it tasted the same way her mouth did when she would bite her lip by mistake. She went back upstairs to read. After moving on from the pyramids she became obsessed with Anne Boleyn. She liked the way Anne disrupted things. She took calculated risks with high stakes in exchange for high rewards, at least that is how Jane interpreted the story. She felt that Anne understood things about how to get those around her to do her will—how to show people what they really wanted—before she understood what the word *manipulation* meant or could mean.

Control was what Jane wanted and would learn to achieve. She learned it first by managing her parents' moods, relaying messages to them when they were fighting, running up and down the stairs to try and calm them down. When alone in her room the noises would float under her door and through the vents. It was during these moments that she would sit on her blue-grey carpet and pick strands of it apart. These sessions would sometimes last for hours. Only when it was over—after she'd failed to keep the peace—would she collect all the pieces of carpet she had destroyed, leave her room, and then count them as she threw them into the small garbage bin near the toilet.

Jane's last day of the workshop leaves her feeling nothing, as she's spent its entirety hungover. There is a blunt goodbye between her and the older participants who she now realizes are her seniors in more ways than one, meaning they've established their own names in the art community while all having families and fulfilling lives. It's like Jane wants to comfort herself by ensuring that she has known more pain than any of them. This can't be the truth, though. Her pain is vapid and ordinary. She doesn't know the others' lives. Jane is the first to leave the room as she mouths *thank you* to the instructor.

The way Jane walks down the hall reminds her of when she used to avoid cracks in the sidewalk as a child. She's wrapping her oversized trench coat around her shoulders while listening to the clap of her heeled boots on the hard floor of the gallery. She'd packed the coat thinking that the weather in London would be warmer than it is in Toronto. It's still not that warm.

Jane feels a distressing urge that she doesn't understand. She has unfinished business. She has to go back. It might have something to do with the want of a connection. It could be a need for feedback, or another concept altogether—that of an expression of gratitude. She turns around and heads back to the classroom. Most of the other participants of the workshop are heading out the door so Jane stalls a bit before going back in. While pretending to look at her phone, she lifts her head briefly to smile at her classmates, who are holding each other as they depart. She will never see them again. She watches them hug each other. Some of them exchange phone numbers. Jane takes it all in, wondering if and how she could possibly care. Once everyone has dispersed, she walks into the classroom with a tepid feeling of vulnerability.

"Hey," she says to the instructor while sitting down on one of the empty chairs.

"Hello, Jane. Thank you for all your good work."

"Was it okay?" Jane feels stupid asking this question because men would not ask this question.

"Jane, do *you* think it was okay?"

"I don't know, and I need someone to tell me."

"You could go your whole life without someone telling you that your work is okay. Are you ready for that?"

Jane starts to pick at the skin under her fingernails. She is no longer in a position to make eye contact with her instructor and the worst part is that she knows why. Jane wants to say the worst thing, to express that she is ready to go a long time without praise. It's not that she thinks she's good enough, more that she is just ready to study and to try to be better. She could probably go on, without praise, forever. She'd rather not, though.

"Thank you," Jane says, not knowing what she's thanking her for or why. The conversation seems like something she will remember, but not for a long time.

She and Kitty are supposed to fly back to Toronto in a week. Jane's barely seen her the whole trip. She's hooked up with a few people whom she barely remembers and possibly hates, gone to many of Justin's parties. Her best time in England has been spent sitting in cold parks and sketching furiously, as if she could somehow hone her skills to equal those of the artists in her workshop in a manner of weeks.

Her impatience shows in her work. Her mind wanders easily to her ruthless obsession with the need to drink. She wants to make Kitty feel guilty for leaving her alone with her art.

Text message to Kitty: *What the fuck are you doing?*

The next day, Kitty returns to the hotel with apology fish and chips. They place their newspaper meals on their laps as they sit together on a stiff green couch. Jane picks at hers.

"Do you want to go to one last party? It's a benefit of some kind."

"We could just get a bottle here. Listen to music?"

"Justin's got my ticket. You may have to buy one, sorry," Kitty says as she throws her newspaper package in the bin. She begins to brush her dark hair in front of the mirror.

"How much?"

"I'm not sure!" Kitty does not seem to understand that they are living beyond their means.

"I see."

"I'll get ready with you."

The next evening, as she waits for Kitty to return to the room, Jane recalls the one time she was alone with Justin. They were waiting for Kitty to come back from a hair appointment he'd paid for. Through the drawn hotel curtains the sun formed doily-flower shapes on the wall behind the table, where they sat sipping the champagne he'd ordered from room service and paid for with cash. When he'd walked to get it, he glided as if he were on ice skates.

"Can I take a photo of you?"

"I'll consider it," Jane replied, deadpan.

"In the bath." Justin's hands were folded together behind his head.

"Why?" Jane wanted to know how this was appealing so she could understand the theme of bath photographs in her life.

"It'll be good."

"You don't even have a camera."

"I have my phone."

"Great."

He pointed to the bathroom. "Go inside and get undressed."

"Really?" But the way she said it made her feel embarrassed.

"There's nothing else to do." He smiled.

Jane walked to the bathroom. Once inside she watched herself in the mirror as she took her clothes off—a black turtleneck, her jean skirt, a pair of tights that had a rip in the crotch—throwing each item out the bathroom door so that Justin could see she was doing it. After tossing a black, sparkling thong over her shoulder and out the door, Jane turned towards the mirror that was lined with exposed filament bulbs in an attempt at some industrial look. Justin was there holding her panties, as if catching them was his plan all along. He wrapped them around the neck of his glass of champagne. A moment passed with only the sound of the bubbles fizzing when they reached the top of Justin's glass. Justin spoke.

"I can't believe you did that."

On the day of the benefit Jane sleeps in late. She wakes up at one in the afternoon, sets an alarm for when she should start getting ready, then goes back to sleep for a few more hours. When her alarm rings she experiences a strong craving for coke to help her wake up, knowing there is a little bit left if only she could remember where she hid it. Justin gave it to them. Jane had dreamed that she was on a table inside of a dark castle. She was being tied up and a bunch of men were taking turns fucking her. Professor Nicolas Price was there, as well as Justin. The strangeness of the dream combined with her desire for it to be real has made it even more difficult for Jane to get out of bed. She'll have to find the cocaine.

Kitty has avoided a number of Jane's phone calls. Jane looks at the liquor stocked in the mini-bar. Her impulse is to make herself a drink while she puts on makeup and listens to music. She pauses, wondering if she really *has* to drink. When this ritual manifested itself. By half-past six she realizes that Kitty is not going to show up.

After applying red lipstick and then rubbing it off, Jane sits on the leather couch and takes photographs of herself but the way she's tilting her head looks awkward. She begins to squat on the couch. She posts the picture on social media and waits to make sure someone likes it in the span of four minutes. If not, it will be taken down.

Jane phones Richard while pouring a drink, counting the time difference with her fingers.

"Kitty ditched me."

"Typical."

"I was supposed to go to this thing with her and this guy she's seeing. She asked me to buy a ticket."

"Did you buy one?"

"Fuck no."

"Who the fuck cares? You're Jane. Go solo. Walk in."

"And pick someone up?" she says as a joke.

"No. Wait for me. Come back to me."

Jane smiles cruelly as she hears this then remembers her own vulnerability. "What if I'm stuck standing alone?"

"Don't those things have free booze?"

"I don't know."

"Go! Sneak in and steal the booze."

"Okay."

"I gotta go. Goodnight!"

Now she remembers where she hid the coke. There's some left inside the Bible in the bedside table. Jane needs more energy, perhaps courage. She calls a minicab, takes two more photographs of herself in the mirror, sends three more text messages to Kitty, and is on her way.

Once she arrives at another hotel, she's denied entry by a woman with a clipboard, then a bouncer. "Darling, you're not wearing the proper clothing. There is a theme. White dresses."

Jane looks inside to see an assortment of dresses that look like they're for a wedding. Jane has promised herself she will never wear shades of white or colour until the day her depression lifts. The gold doorway is decorated with ivory roses and subtle, flashing fairy lights. Kitty didn't even tell her how to dress.

Jane is drunk when she sends her last message to Kitty: *Why didn't you like my selfie, you careerist fuck.*

nine

A younger Jane used to walk to the corner store near her house and buy chocolate bars with the Spice Girls stamped onto them. She'd often take bites out of the rectangular chocolate bars in order to trace out the shape of each singer, taking little nibbles around the microphones that they were holding. The kids would trade the chocolate bars as well as Spice Girls gum, bought with pennies, that came with a sticker inside. Everyone had their favourite, and the stickers were often traded for ones with a more popular Spice Girl on them.

They were touring, and the concert near Jane's town was taking place in two weeks. She had gone on the internet to see if someone was selling their ticket. She didn't really know how to use the internet, though, and although she'd stolen her mother's credit card to make the purchase, she didn't get far. She managed to get some pictures of the singers to come up on the screen and she clicked on a photo, thinking this must be the way to order tickets. Over and over she clicked. There was an option to leave a message in the guest book, above all the photos of the beautiful members of the band. The guest book was a tab on the website where people could comment on what they had seen, leave their mark. Jane scrolled through some of the messages—things like "great fan site! I love the spice girls 2!" and "Posh is my favourite what's urs?!"

Jane held her mother's credit card in her hand as she thought about what to type. As she traced her fingers over the bumps of the card number, she noticed that the colour was worn out and that there were scratches all along the thick black line on the back. Jane wanted to see the Spice Girls more than anything. She typed a comment in the guest book: "please send me 1 ticket" and then typed out every word and number she could find on the card followed by "thank u." She pressed the button underneath the comment box. *Submit.*

For the next week Jane volunteered to fetch the mail from the post-office box. She'd jog to the mailbox, which was around the corner—past Hannah's as well as the weird man's house—hoping to find a ticket to her dream show. Hearing those songs live would make Jane feel like she was understood.

After shuffling through the letters and leafing through some of the grocery store flyers, she walked home, disappointed but not defeated. On her way she noticed the weird man sitting on his roof drinking a large can of an adult drink. He waved it in her direction and yelled her name in a conspicuous way even though she was across the road. Jane felt embarrassed; she didn't want Hannah or any of the other kids around the neighbourhood knowing that the weird guy knew her name. She'd have wondered what he was doing up there if it were not for the ladder and the tool box he was sitting next to.

She went to call on Hannah. Her mother answered, in her white tennis outfit. Jane wanted to be as pretty as Hannah's mom when she grew up.

"Hi, Jane. How is your poor mother?"

"What's wrong with my mom?"

"Oh! I just got off the phone with her. Her credit card has been compromised."

"What does that mean?"

"It means that someone found out your mother's credit card number and has been buying stuff while pretending to be her."

"That's not good."

"Not at all. Hopefully she gets her money back soon."

"She can get her money back?"

"Yes, Jane. These are all adult things." Hannah's mom checked her gold watch. "What was it you wanted?"

"Is Hannah home?"

"Not right now, she's getting her hair dyed for a shoot."

"But she's eight years old."

"I'll tell her you came by."

Jane put her hands in her shorts pockets and turned to walk down Hannah's driveway, past the two SUVs that her mom and dad owned.

"Wait," Hannah's mom yelled, still standing in the doorway.

Jane walked back to the door, pausing when Hannah's mom signalled with her finger—*one minute*. She came back with an envelope and started counting what was inside.

"My husband doesn't want to go see the Spice Girls," she said.

"Who wouldn't want to see the Spice Girls!"

"Would you like to come with Hannah and me? I'll have to make sure it's okay with your mother."

"I'd love to!" Jane replied, thinking briefly about whether Hannah would even want her to go and then not caring. This was her free ride.

On the night of the show Jane was opening a jar of body glitter and listening to a CD on the tiny blue player that she'd got for Christmas. She heard her mother calling from down the stairs that Jane was going to be late but Jane lingered because she wanted to look pretty in case she met the members of the group. To Jane, the Spice Girls represented happiness and fun. They did whatever they wanted but what she admired most of all was their work ethic. They were always touring and always together. Jane wanted to have a friendship—a group—like the Spice Girls had with each other. But she didn't think she looked good. At least not the way that Hannah always did. The glitter that she had slathered all over her face and body was starting to sting in places. Around her face and under her kneecaps. She went into her mother's room and found her makeup bag, sorting through the items, not knowing what each of them did. She chose a large tube of a substance that was thick. It read *concealer*. She put some on her hand and then all over her face. Then she took some pink stuff and put it on her cheeks the same way she had watched her mother do so many times.

Jane heard a call from downstairs, "Hannah is here!" She put the makeup back in the bag exactly as she found it.

When she walked down the stairs her mother sighed. She told Jane to wait there and went into the other room, calling for Jane's father.

"Can you please tell her not to go through my makeup bag?" Jane didn't really understand why her mother was talking about her like she wasn't there.

"Jane, your mother's makeup is very expensive."

"I think I look ugly."

"I'll have to hide it," her mother said to no one in particular.

It was a short trip to the amphitheatre in Toronto. The highways were empty because the commuters had already gone home for the day. Jane sat in the back seat of the car listening to Hannah and her mother chat about firing Hannah's agent.

"But isn't she your friend?" Hannah asked her mother timidly.

"She'll get over it."

Hannah's mom kept one hand on the wheel while she rifled through the glove compartment for a flip-book full of pocket sleeves with CDs inside. She handed it to her daughter.

"What would you like to listen to?"

Hannah chose a Spice Girls CD. She and Jane sang along the rest of the way.

The concert was busy. It took them about half an hour to wade through the crowd outside and get their tickets scanned. Hannah and her mom walked calmly ahead of her. Her mom stopped in line at a concession stand.

"What would you like to drink, dear?" she asked Jane.

"A Coke, please."

She ordered a Coke and a bottle of water, which she handed to her daughter. Hannah took the water and opened the lid, sipping carefully as if she didn't want a single drop to fall to the floor.

They found their seats. Jane went in first, nestling in between Hannah and another group. The group on her left were older, wearing belly tube-tops and pink lipstick.

"How did you get the tickets?" Jane tried to lean across Hannah a bit to speak to her mom.

"Hannah's father gets tickets for everything through his work."

Jane sat back down in her seat and grabbed her friend's arm. "Lucky!"

She was ready to dance and sing. To scream and try to get the group to notice her even though they would be far away from her on the stage that was slowly being set up.

"I wonder what they're going to wear," Hannah said to Jane.

"Something like what you're wearing." Jane's friend had her hair in pigtails that fell onto a light blue dress with spaghetti straps. Not the sole copied outfit of Baby Spice in the arena.

"I'm Baby!" She started yelling until her mother told her to be quiet.

If Jane was invited to play Spice Girls, she was usually told to be Ginger Spice because of her freckles. That was fine, Ginger Spice also went by Sexy Spice and although Jane didn't know what "sexy" really meant—or how to be that— she hoped that she would get there.

The Spice Girls were taking their time. The opener had already performed—a dreamy singer whose lyrics focused on her time spent in bars. Jane's mom had given her forty dollars for the show so that Jane could buy some snacks and a Spice Girls t-shirt. Hannah and her mom were looking at some magazine clippings that Hannah's mom had pulled out of her bag.

"Jane, look at my model!"

Jane stretched her body over the arm of her seat, not before taking in the ways Hannah and her mom resembled each other. She wondered if she dressed her daughter so that she could look similar to her or if it was the other way around. Hannah's mom was holding pictures of Hannah cut out from the magazine. She was modelling a variety of outfits for the children's section of the Sears catalogue. In the photo she was grinning as if she had come out of the womb smiling the exact same way; it was a smile that was ready— like Hannah was—for gifts and praise.

"You look so pretty!"

"She does!" Hannah's mom kissed her daughter on the cheek.

"Seriously, you look like you could be a Spice Girl."

"I'm Baby Spice." Hannah now spoke in a slow tone as if the duty of being Baby Spice was a punishing burden.

"Is it all right if I go to the bathroom?" Jane asked Hannah's mom. Jane wanted to go buy a t-shirt but she knew that such an errand would be too much for a small child to do alone. She was determined to go on an adventure.

While Hannah's mom was showing the woman next to her the photos, Jane saw an opportunity. She left without waiting for a response—motioning to Hannah in the direction of a washroom sign.

The crowd in the hallway of the amphitheatre was larger than when she'd arrived, consisting mostly of grownups who didn't notice her. Occasionally, she'd see a child her age but she was left wondering why there weren't more young people here. She just wanted to find the t-shirt stand. To find a shirt with a picture of all the Spice Girls on it so that she could look cool at school.

There was a lounge area with a bunch of older people in it. They were drinking from plastic cups with little lids on them that reminded Jane of a sippy cup. The liquid was a light brown colour Jane recognized—beer.

She went into the area to ask where the t-shirts were being sold. She hadn't asked Hannah to come with her because she was sick of the way Hannah dominated things. It was relatively easy for Jane to wish she looked more like her friend. Jane had a lot of freckles and she hated them. Hannah was a beautiful model, in Sears catalogues everywhere.

Jane tried to think of good things about herself. She was a better reader than Hannah, but other than that, she felt dull compared to her glamorous neighbour.

She sat on a bench beside two teenagers who were comparing driver's licenses while exchanging shrill bursts of laughter. They were wearing cut-up Spice Girls shirts that showed their belly buttons, with bell-bottom jeans. They looked cool.

"I got mine from that place downtown," said one of the girls who had her long brown hair in a slicked-back ponytail with two different-coloured scrunchies.

"Everyone knows about that place, though," another girl said. "Don't bouncers look out for that?"

"They didn't this time," she laughed and she fell over a bit, balancing herself on her friend's shoulder. "Where did you get yours?"

"My boyfriend gave it to me." The other girl shrugged. Jane didn't know why they were comparing driver's licenses or why they were laughing about it. Then there was an announcement on the speaker: *Please find your seats. The show will begin shortly.*

The people next to her left quickly.

One of them left their sippy cup of beer behind. Jane picked it up and drank from it. Jane was thirsty but she also felt lonely. She drank some more from the cup and didn't feel anything from it.

She realized that she wasn't going to get a t-shirt. It wasn't worth missing the Spice Girls. When she stood up, she felt a warm feeling coming from her stomach. She felt good as she began to wade through the crowd. She started pushing at people who were in her way and most of them moved when they saw her.

When she reached her seat, a chant had formed in the stadium. Everyone was yelling for the Spice Girls to come onstage.

If Hannah's mom had noticed how long she was gone, she didn't say anything. She was deep in conversation with the woman next to her, who looked her age. Hannah was standing and sing-shouting, her body leaning against the rail in front of their seats. Her back was to Jane.

Jane kept eyeing the modelling photos that lay discarded like playing cards in a poker game. Jane joined in the chant, her voice barely audible over that of the crowd. Hannah's mom was still talking to their neighbour.

It didn't take much time for Jane to pick up the clippings. She paused for a moment before ripping the first one—a picture of Hannah wearing a pink raincoat. One by one she ripped them and only when her feet were surrounded by little pieces of magazine did she look up to notice Hannah's mom staring at her with an expression that was a mixture of repulsion, pity, and rage.

A couple of weeks later there was a For Sale sign on Hannah's lawn. It seemed unlikely that they would move because of the incident at the concert, although the thought did cross Jane's mind. They were probably just too fancy for the neighbourhood.

Jane walked to the door. She peeked through the blinds in the window beside the door and saw Hannah talking to her mom while she mixed a salad. Jane rang the doorbell, stepping back on the porch so that she was farther away, hoping they hadn't seen her peeking in.

It took a while for Hannah's mom to answer the door and Jane thought she heard a big "shush."

"Hello, Jane," Hannah's mom said, pausing afterward as if she expected Jane to explain her presence.

"Is Hannah home?"

"Not at the moment, dear." Jane didn't know if she should explain that she'd just seen Hannah in the kitchen.

"Are you sure?" Jane could see Hannah's head popping out of the hallway behind her mom. She was snickering.

She let out a deep breath. "Yes, I'm sure."

On the way home Jane felt defeated. Why didn't Hannah want to see her? She suspected it had something to do with the ripped photos—maybe Hannah's mom thought that Jane was some sort of disturbed child.

A voice called to her. It was the man who sat on his roof sometimes. He was leaning on his car with a large bottle of something on the hood next to him.

"Come here," he said. "I have something to show you."

The bottle he had was different this time, one with thick amber liquid inside. Everything smelled strong. He rummaged in his pocket and brought out a tube of toothpaste. He started putting dabs of toothpaste on each of his fingers as Jane watched. Then he said, "Look, it's candy."

"No, it's not," Jane said flatly. "It's toothpaste."

"When you put it on your fingers it turns into candy." At this point he had toothpaste on each finger of his right hand, except the pinky finger. Jane could see the ribbon of red inside of the white paste, the ribbon that only shows up when you have pushed the toothpaste out perfectly so that it looks the same as in the commercial.

"I don't want any," she said.

"Just try some. I told you it turns into candy once it's on my fingers."

"What?"

"Something to drink, then?"

"No, I don't want your germs."

The man who liked to sit on the roof started talking to someone who wasn't there. "She doesn't want my germs!" he said, laughing hard.

People with low serotonin are more likely to feel they've been treated unfairly and to seek revenge.

Jane stretches her neck as if she's waking up for the first time in years. Languid and sardonic, it takes her three minutes to realize she's left the bench where she was sitting and shaking. She is now walking down to the river. She hates the tourists' riverbank even though she is a tourist herself, but it's tolerable tonight. Empty like she's at a carnival after everyone has gone home. She passes the Ferris wheel that is actually called the London Eye. She's swigging whiskey, taking in the deserted, gated entrance where people pay and line up to ride. She remembers being on the London Eye as a child with a distant relative and her fiancé while watching them make out.

"Your parents don't do this, do they?" her voice had goaded, as if she expected Jane to lie and say they did.

Standing in the futuristic-looking pod, Jane didn't know how to respond to her. She remembered the arguments that occurred after the two bottles of wine her parents split every dinner. The fights revolved around money and around Jane, for causing unknown trouble.

Jane spends another hour ducking into alleys and checking for cameras before she swigs from her bottle. She doesn't want to be seen doing it, and the mixture of whatever she's on is making her feel paranoid, like all the cameras are watching her. She's still wearing her black dress with the slit on the side of the leg and she feels beautiful, like a tragic prom queen who's been stood up. She checks her purse for leftover uppers. One left. If she takes it now, she may still sleep tonight. It's only one in the morning. She takes half the pill, planning to take the other half wherever she ends up next.

There are lights flashing from a large building in the sky like there's a party happening, but she's still too far away to see.

Do people throw parties around here? Would it be good?

Jane walks towards the light.

She takes the second half of her last pill and is thankful the bars don't close early here. She's left bits of herself everywhere since she was born. Feeling nothing is a full-time job. She accepts that her ability to feel has been gone for a long time but maybe it was stolen from her. Maybe by Kitty. Possibly even by Justin, Richard, or someone else. She might not remember.

Anna claims that Jane's memories—the ones that come like spears in her chest—are not true to what really happened. They're warped by her shame, guilt, hopes, her perception of who she is. Anna tells Jane she is an all-or-nothing thinker.

Outside the doors, a bouncer stands smoking with some men in suits. Jane can't remember what has brought her here. Maybe her feet, physically, and maybe anger. She approaches the men, seeing herself through a camera lens. She imagines the reactions of her parents (indifferent), Anna (concerned), Kitty (amused) and Richard (?).

"Are you alone?" This man's angled features seem like a caricature, or it could be the way that his hair is slicked back. Jane allows him to light a cigarette for her and as he does so she imagines his entire childhood. She assumes boarding school. She's seen him so many times. She looks at the stubble that he's probably spent a while maintaining, his bemused expression. She's indifferent to what her impulsive brain has already set her up to do.

"I'm always alone. What's up there?"

"Wouldn't you like to know." She likes this man's disdain. It hardly matters. She simply wants a warm body while she comes down from her high, so she can stop thinking about Kitty's rejection and stop thinking about anything.

She spends the rest of her time in England wandering. She visits art galleries, gardens, bridges, whispering to herself as if Kitty or Richard were there. She ignores calls from the man she met the night she spent at the river. Jane had returned to the hotel to find all of Kitty's belongings gone.

She is reluctant to phone Anna because she's embarrassed. Jane doesn't know if it was her drinking or some sort of deep-seated personality flaw that led Kitty to leave. Kitty could be some kind of sociopath. Apparently, psychopaths are born that way and sociopaths go through something that makes them that way. Jane could be in the process of becoming one. The call goes to Anna's voicemail.

The afternoon before they are supposed to fly home, Jane takes one last walk downtown to say goodbye to this city that gives her a different feeling, if not still a lonely one. She's been calling Kitty at random intervals since she vanished. She's shocked when she finally gets through.

"Hey," Kitty answers in a different, raspier voice than Jane is used to. She offers no apology for her disappearance.

"We're supposed to leave tomorrow."

"Okay."

"We came together and barely hung out. Are you planning on returning to Toronto?"

"I'm really sick of your emotional manipulation, Jane. Justin says it's toxic."

"Of course he does." Jane feels faint. She might be hungry. "What do you mean, *manipulation*?"

"I think you do it without realizing."

"I don't think so."

"Justin says you asked him to take pictures of you."

"He asked me."

"That's not what he says."

"He's the one who's manipulative."

"I have to go."

"Of course you do."

Jane puts her phone in her back pocket. She thumbs through her purse and finds a ten-pound note. She could buy some fries at McDonald's, or an energy bar somewhere. She needs water so she heads towards Trafalgar Square so she can rest in the National Gallery. She detests public water fountains because the spout is always too close to the bottom of the basin and she's petrified her mouth will accidentally touch part of the metal. It's about germs. She doesn't want them. When she finally finds one, in the basement of the gallery, a man is brushing his teeth and spitting into it. Had she stumbled upon this fountain two minutes later she wouldn't have seen the man and would have drunk from it. Her para-noia would have stopped her mouth from touching the spout and everything would have been fine, but somehow seeing the man and hearing him spit into the fountain is enough to put her off drinking from it. This whole rejection of the foun-tain makes her feel terrible, like a more brilliant, kinder person would have found a way around it, or would have put their face in the toothpaste. It's too much for her to bear.

She has to check her bank account to see if she can afford three medium-sized bottles of whiskey from the store. One for her present reality, one for the night, and one to down before she gets on the plane tomorrow morning. She tries not to think about the fact that she refuses to spend money on food and water and once she looks, she knows she's going to have to see if someone will wire her money. She might have to ask Richard. Anna—she could ask but there will be some hesitancy from her end. Anna has something better than money, though. She has the great answer Jane craves. There is a question Jane is on the verge of asking herself about loneliness.

In the end it's Richard who transfers her the money. She takes the whiskey home with her to pack.

When the times comes, she's lucid enough to take public transit to the station then transfer to a different train that goes to the airport. She's finished two of the three bottles and she knows that the third won't make it through customs, so she downs as much as she can while she smokes her last cigarette before the plane, careful to avoid cameras and any sort of security. It doesn't really matter. She's sneaky when it comes to drinking in public. Her most famous move, or motto, is to be hidden in plain sight. Anyone who saw her drinking from a bottle of whiskey outside an airport would be sure that they imagined it. They would question their own reality, not Jane's.

Near the end of the plane ride, she selects an hour-long ambient electronic mix to last for the rest of the journey. Drone music that will allow her to rest deep inside her internal world. A world that is one of beauty and gaps. Many things she can't remember and won't. It takes her about twenty minutes of the mix to find a comfortable position to rest in. When she settles in, feet dangling out into the aisle in the way they tell you not to, her face pushed against a small pillow gifted by the airline, everything feels dead and right.

ten

Jane is sitting on her pullout couch picking feathers from the paisley throw pillow next to her. She's fucked up her black nail polish. She knows a woman of secrets must always have dark nails. This air of mystery can only be upheld if she has any secrets and if people care about her at all.

A message from Anna flashes on her phone. She needs to ignore her today because Anna is trying to lift the depression Jane has become accustomed to since she came home. It nurtures her, reminding her that she is the smartest, and that her pain makes her special. Jane is having trouble getting out of bed, and she feels guilty for being irritated by the one person who is trying to help her. She's asking Jane to do things like reach out to an old friend. But Anna keeps insisting that she provide evidence, like a screenshot of the message from a friend or a photo of the park across the street to prove she's left bed. She hoped something good would happen in London but it turns out she was just a drunk in a different country.

"I know it's hurtful when someone distances themselves," Anna said about Kitty last time they spoke. Jane hadn't thought that her mood could get any worse. Her numbness is expertly maintained, but there is a deep pang of melancholy that can slip in at any moment.

She sent Kitty a bunch of mean texts while drunk a week ago. Kitty replied reaffirming Jane's own toxicity as a friend. She's embarrassed that she lashed out. She hates how modern technology mixed with her poor impulse control can make a situation worse in seconds.

She phones Richard. When he picks up he sounds like he's out of breath.

"*Bonjour.*" Jane lowers her voice when she speaks on the phone.

"Getting changed. I'm sweating."

"You work out?"

"I tried to go for a jog. I might die."

"Try not to."

"I'll come over?" he asks. Jane is pleased with his eagerness.

"Yes, bring whiskey." She hopes her voice doesn't betray any desperation of her own. "I already have some."

———

While they listen to repetitive electronic music, Richard tries to persuade Jane to mix the whiskey with lemonade, but she pours it into a glass of ice. The bad thoughts are coming quickly. Thoughts that weave a tapestry of failure and indecision. She can be her most gloomy, fucked-up self with Richard. She needs the attention, hoping it means she looks better than she thinks she does, than she feels. Sometimes Jane stares at Richard sleeping and wonders what he wants with her. What they get from each other. One minute he's telling his ridiculous stories, the next he's whipping her in bed, sullen and almost bored like someone who's done it many times before. Neither Jane nor Richard has the emotional vulnerability for a legitimate relationship. It's something Jane wants. Though, if there were any possibility she could get to a point where she was meeting herself with kindness, she would feel even more boring than she does now.

As Jane continues to pick the black nail polish off, she can feel the thin protective layer of her nail peel away with the strong adhesive that binds the lacquer to her fingers. Richard talks about inane subjects like where he parks his car and his fight with his landlord. She feels her mind splitting into two parts. One that can internally apologize for her own negative thinking, and one that can listen to Richard while answering with a gentle rephrasing of his complaints to prove she's listening. Does he notice her disparate selves? Jane concentrates on trying to get out of her own head. She digs her fingernail into her arm until there are little red half-moons nestled between her freckles, which are fading due to lack of sun.

By the time he pulls out the drugs, Jane is on her way to being a bit fucked. Her mind is on secrets again. She needs a new one. Richard places them on the table in triumph like he is a hunter who's just brought home a rare find.

"What is it?"

"Acid."

"What a wonderful idea." She can pretend that Richard, along with the acid, is a teacher or a therapist who is going to cure Jane of her melancholy.

"You'll be good if I'm here," he says, as he turns off his phone and puts a blank notebook on the table. "In case we get inspired."

"Wait, are we doing it here? In my apartment?"

"For your first time, yes." He doesn't want to wander the streets with Jane on acid. It could be worse than drunk Jane. Richard takes his and Jane watches. She copies his exact movements when it's her turn.

"How do you know it's my first time? Aren't we supposed to be like, in a forest?"

"That's how I know. Now turn off your phone."

———

184

Half an hour later, Jane thinks Richard is playing a practical joke on her.

"Relax. Something will be different," Richard says with a gentle seriousness.

This conversation reverberates until Jane begins to notice the picture on Richard's sock. A man with grey hair. She knows who it is, but she can't grasp the name of the man.

"I have paranoia issues."

"Maybe you should be medicating for that."

"I can't come because of the antidepressants I have to take." She paces back and forth, wondering if she should have done anything to the room before they got high.

"Yes, you can."

"Not really."

"Which ones? Let me search the internet to make sure they're okay with acid."

Jane wonders what searching the internet for this information will do now. She's already taken it. Yet Richard appears calm and responsible. Jane feels her chest burn with warmth towards him because of his futile concern.

"It's a bit too late."

"You'll be okay."

"We're fucked."

"If anything happens, I will wrap you in a warm blanket."

Jane has a picture of a ballerina on her wall, one she didn't paint herself. It's an Edgar Degas painting that Kitty once told her is embarrassing. It does not start to dance like she expects it to. Jane realizes that no drug is better than alcohol, but she wants to make sure. She feels like dancing. She squeaks about how amazing everything is.

"Your voice has risen significantly." Richard's words come out slowly.

"I feel like a jellyfish." Jane starts dancing. Her movements are languid, as if she were wading in water.

"I'd like to be filmed underwater," Jane continues. In the mirror, she notices that one of her eyes is turned sideways. It's back to normal when she gets closer. She puts her arms in the air. She knows she's a jellyfish.

"Please lower your voice." Richard is doodling in the book he laid out. He's drawing a picture of a man howling into nothing.

"I think it would be fun. We should make a movie."

"How long can you hold your breath for?"

"I'm not sure."

"You can only be filmed underwater for as long as you can hold your breath."

Jane decides that her companion is being a complete asshole and continues to act out her destiny as a jellyfish. She tries to do a sexy jellyfish dance and sways her ass to one side while she takes a pen and jabs it into the wall.

"Richard! Pay attention to me."

"What?"

"Who do you think you are."

"Just me."

"You're the most simple man I've ever dated. Do you know who I am?"

"Stop being annoying." Richard seems sober and impatient. Jane doesn't know why he's not angry about being called boring. Maybe he just finds it hilarious, or he couldn't care less what Jane thinks. Richard lies down in the bed. Jane settles herself on her back on the floor with her legs stretched up the wall. The stretch feels good. They lie in silence for a while until Richard jerks out of bed as if someone has given him an electric shock. He finds Jane's computer and opens it—tapping at the keyboard with just one finger as if each key is a sensitive button.

"Did you change your password?"

"Yes."

"Why? You don't trust me?"

"No, the computer made me change it."

"What's the password?"

"Jane12345."

"Nice."

Richard walks over to the wall where Jane is and she swings her legs down so they are sitting cross-legged, side by side. They search the internet for 'fun facts about jellyfish' and read that they glow in the dark and can clone themselves. Each new revelation brings Jane to hilarious tears. Their conversation feels like an hour but is only twenty minutes. Jane feels like smashing things then jumping off a cliff, so she tries to stop the feeling by lighting a cigarette. It's not enough. The word for the feeling might be pain.

Richard moves closer and touches her elbow. He tells her it's too dry and she'll never be happy if her elbow is so dry. They start to kiss on the floor by the wall.

The sex is rather clinical. She fakes an orgasm, which is something she rarely even bothers to do. The faking of the orgasm is so pathetic that she begins to sob while his penis is inside of her. He sighs and starts to stroke her hair. Jane can't see his face but she is certain that he's rolling his eyes.

Jane would have slept all the next day if Richard hadn't woken her up.

"Jane. Get up, hurry!" He talks as if there is some kind of emergency.

"What's up?"

"Nothing, I was just bored." He's holding two disposable coffee cups with pink lids. There is a bag with a croissant sticking out of it, held between two of his fingers and looking like it is about to drop. Americanos and a chocolate croissant.

Jane buries her face in the pillow, ignoring Richard. It's that moment in the morning when she remembers Kitty's blatant using of her and the time they wasted together.

She turns to Richard. "I need a female friend."

"Am I not enough?"

"Marry me."

"No."

Jane scrunches her face together while staring at a dead pigeon in the gutter. She feels like she might vomit. Food will help. Richard always buys brunch when they're hungover.

"This is it."

It's been a few weeks since their time on acid and Richard seems to have brushed off the crying sex. They're drinking together again because Jane has no one else. Richard seems happy with it. Jane can't remember the last day she went without a drink.

"Not ironic enough," he says after studying the pigeon for a minute.

"Fuck you."

"Maybe if it was wearing a party hat."

The streets are so empty she expects a tumbleweed to roll past them. They have spent the whole morning searching for music, objects, and people they can associate with their newly coined term to cover things that seem morbidly strange. Jane will later find out that many people use the term *Lynchian*, and she'll be disappointed because she thought she and Richard were geniuses. Richard has known all along so she is alone in her shame. Later she reads that David Foster Wallace described *Lynchian* as "a particular kind of irony where the very macabre and the very mundane combine in such a way as to reveal the former's perpetual containment within the latter."

Jane pulls her hair into a French braid but wispy strands fall out, which she thinks must make her look mad. Richard is faring better so he gets to be the leader for the day. He's chosen to wear tight black pants and a black V-neck that he scooped from Jane's floor. He's playing with a purple yo-yo with the skill of someone who has been trained since childhood.

"Is it almost eleven?" Jane lights her second cigarette of the morning, which is an improvement.

"Let's just chill out and eat." Richard winds the string back into his yo-yo.

"I want one of those ten-percent beers."

The pub is empty. They make their way to the back so they can sit in their favourite private cubby. It's in a closed-off room where no one can bother them. There are framed pictures of owls and foxes above a bench lined with red velvet. Jane feels ill so she constructs a bed for herself out of bar stools and stares at Richard's hopeful face as he slides her a menu.

"What do you want? My treat." Richard watches her as she lifts the plastic laminated menu and looks at what kind of nachos they have. She's more interested in the beer.

An older-looking server stands impatiently in the doorway, tall with grey hair and quite slim.

"We'll have two Delirium." Richard likes to order for her. The server nods and looks bored but doesn't tell them to leave the closed-off room. They sit in silence until their beers arrive. Jane takes a sip, puts the beer down, picks it up a moment later, and takes two gulps.

"These are good," says Richard, nodding.

"Our server is kind of hot."

"You would."

"This song could be in a David Lynch film."

"Yeah, it's sort of lo-fi and eerie, I guess. Synthy."

"What's it called?" Jane asks.

"Dare you to ask the server."

"I'm too shy. Probably hates us already for sitting in this room so far in the back." Jane plays with the green paint stain on her black pants. She swigs the last of her beer. The morning alcohol mixed with the cigarettes is enough to make her feel sensible.

Ever since Kitty's harsh rejection, Jane feels as though she is in a special club set apart from the rest of her self-respecting peers, the club of those who don't need to be cared for. It's like this inherent need for attention, stimulation, inebriation, and oblivion is all she cares to explore. If someone asked her what she would do instead of this—the feeling—she wouldn't have a clue.

But for now everything is chill and good. She and Richard have not been fighting much, and he is being less of a fuck-ass mainly because he isn't accusing her of not being nice to his cat. Maybe he can sense a shift in Jane. She is beginning to care less about everything.

Jane pulls out her cell phone and opens up a video that she has been meaning to show Richard. "Let's go to this sex club."

Richard leans in. "Jane, you can be a bit shallow at times."

"Pardon me?"

"I consider you the most shallow person I know. Even more than me."

"What does that have to do with anything?"

"Nothing. So, you have never been to a sex club and you want to go."

"Yeah."

"To swim in the pool?"

"There's a pool?"

"You want me to go with you, show you around the sex club, then fuck you on a sofa in front of a group of people?"

"I think it'll be fun. Anyone can watch."

"Maybe. I don't not want that."

"Then why don't we?"

"Just find someone else. You understand that there are a variety of apps that you can use? And how is this all so wild to you? You don't think I know what you do with Kitty and those random people that you meet?"

"*Did* with Kitty."

"You'll do anything as long as there are drugs involved."

"That seems like a harsh judgement."

The server pops his head in and it looks like it's floating amongst the decorations. "How is everything?"

"May we please have two more Delirium?" Jane feels naive and embarrassed after listening to Richard. They sit for a while, Jane playing with the menu until she eventually grabs what's left of Richard's beer because she can't wait for her own to come.

"Hooking up with strangers is fine," Richard finally says. "But I see this impulse coming from a place where you want to distance yourself from a connection. It is a harsh cruelty that you have committed to, one that's self-inflicted." Richard doesn't make eye contact.

"Relax. You're the one who brings me random psychedelics."

"Psychedelics are good for you. You just had a bad time. You need to surround yourself with people who know your darkness." The server returns with two beers, hurrying past them in a way that makes Jane wonder if he's on coke, or just eager to avoid the tension in the room. Jane and Richard each take a sip in silence, at the same time. Then they look at each other and clink their glasses. A new song is playing, a popular one that Jane imagines a happy person would listen to with a certain amount of earnestness. Richard begins to tear up a beer coaster.

"It's. So. Fucking. Annoying. When people do that."

"I forgot you worked in bars."

"Is it possible you're jealous?"

"I rarely get jealous or threatened," Richard says in a flat, bored tone.

Lately Jane has been feeling more dissociated than ever, like she's in a movie. It happens when she zones out and watches people interact and express enthusiasm she doesn't understand. Whenever she's at school, she feels like she's in a film about desperate art students. When she waited tables, she felt like she was in a film about a woman who works at a diner—something like *Twin Peaks*. When she sits in this cubby with Richard, she knows she's in a movie about two sad characters who are pretending they are in a David Lynch film.

Richard takes a long sip of the strong beer then writes something down, folding the napkin into a paper airplane that more closely resembles a crumpled paper ball. He throws it at Jane. The napkin hits her nose and bounces onto the table, narrowly missing her glass of beer. She opens the napkin that turns out to be lined with imprints of swans, anticipating some sort of poem that Richard may have just thought of. The writing on the napkin reads: *fuck me, slut*.

Jane now understands what Richard tried to explain to her a few days ago at the pub. She can use an app. She's already on them. There are many couples online looking for a third. Couples that post pictures of both parties, usually looking boring and posed. Richard and Jane will often laugh at their expense. It's cruel, laughing at a random couple's earnest desperation, and in the end, who is more eager for an experience, these posing couples or Jane? She can make them happy. She can help the world in this small way.

She is naive. Richard is right. She flips through pictures in search of a couple that look like they don't love each other. It's interesting to her that many of the photos involve weddings, sports outings, and treasured moments between two life partners. She settles on one profile that doesn't show either of their faces. There are limited pictures but they are both well dressed. She doesn't want to sleep with anyone who wears an ill-fitting suit.

Jane writes *Hello* and tries to force herself to cry at the thought of a bad suit. How the men who wear them look proud but are missing the allure they are desperately grasping at. Her attempt to feel is interrupted by a notification on her phone.

Hey r u hot?

Before replying, Jane takes a moment to text acquaintances to ask if she is hot. Their responses vary, leaving Jane more confused than before: *be well; my girlfriend saw that; are you okay with yourself?*

Jane has these bird-shaped decoration mirrors in her apartment and she catches her own dead eyes in the bit of glass. She can't look away, opening her eyes as wide as she can until she looks like some deranged rag doll. She hasn't cried since her acid trip with Richard.

—*Yes*, Jane types.

Send pic

—*How tall are you?*

Send pic

—*No.*

Send pic.

She doesn't want this stranger to have her picture. She ends up posing in front of the large standing mirror in her room and taking a photo of herself wearing her nightdress with her face cut out. She agrees to meet them that evening at a bar where she knows everyone and sends a message to Richard reminding him that he's agreed to hold a stakeout, just in case.

I never agreed to that. You're fine. Have fun, he replies.

A couple minutes later he adds, *I want to fuck you after*.

In the shower, Jane leans her head against the wall and stares at the tiles. They're grey, with tiny blue flowers that look like they'd be painted on a teapot. She stands there until the heat makes her feel like she's about to pass out.

She doesn't bother moisturizing but rubs a tinted CC cream on her face and puts a bit of mascara over her blonde eyelashes. She knows Richard will wake her up when he arrives—he wants to wait for her in her apartment—so she lies on her bed and spreads her wet hair all around her head like she's Ophelia in the painting. She sleeps.

"Here." Richard places a paper bag on the table and walks into the other room. His detachment makes Jane wonder if he really cares for her. She picks up a black dress from her floor, wishing she had a pink one or something that would make her feel like she is pretending more.

"For after." Richard has taken one of the giant freezies that Jane keeps in her freezer for when she's hungover and her blood sugar feels fucked up. He rips the top off the bag of orange ice with his teeth.

"Okay." Jane doesn't look in the paper bag because she's scared it will make her seem eager but she assumes it's drugs—coke, hopefully. She is considering asking Richard directly what's inside until she's interrupted.

"I have to make a call," he says as he walks towards the front door.

When Richard returns, his face is distant and dreamlike. "Jane, turns out I can't stay tonight."

"Why?"

"There's this cute girl, and you know."

"You're ditching me? After everything we've been through?"

"Relax, you'll have fun."

"Fuck me after?"

"That's my line." He places a cigarette in his mouth and holds his hand in the air while he leaves like he's waving good-bye to a large crowd. The bag is still on the table.

Jane walks into the bar and greets the bouncer who looks at her with sadness, or at least that is the way Jane perceives it. She picks at the skin underneath her fingernails, a habit she thought she'd grown out of. She can tell the person she's there to meet is the man who has situated himself right by the door—he has grey-blonde hair and is dressed in leather boots with tight jeans, with a blue suit jacket. He's with a woman who has hair that's long enough to look good in a high pony-tail that falls down her back.

"Hey, Jane?" the man makes a show of getting up from his chair. Then he sits back down as Jane approaches, waiting for her to initiate some non-verbal cue confirming it is in fact her and that everything is okay. Jane was worried he was going to hug her. He pulls out a bar stool and motions for Jane to hand over her coat. It is snowing tonight, the first of the year, and Jane is wearing a large wool coat that goes down to her ankles. As Jane sits, his partner's eyes capture every-thing with no indication of any feeling. She studies Jane a moment longer, sipping on a glass of white wine in a drawn-out, surreal way that plays into the reoccurring theme of

Jane's life where she thinks she is in a movie. The two of them are very attractive. She's suspicious of why they were even on the app. Maybe they were bored. When the woman is finished studying her, she turns her head until her chin is sticking out a bit, meeting her partner's eyes in the kind of unspoken communication that Jane has always dreamed of having with another person. The woman never smiles as they chat at the bar and won't during the entirety of their encounter.

"We can go soon," the man says flatly.

"I thought you'd be taller." Jane doesn't know where they are going.

"I'm Blair. This is another Jane."

She continues to chat nervously with the couple inside the cab they're taking to a hotel on Queen West, answering the man's questions honestly and with few words. She probably would have just gone to their house, but Jane guesses they have some reason for booking a hotel. She has a strong inclination to know what Kitty is doing at this very moment.

Everything inside the hotel room is an eggshell white, the decoration sterile, pure, and beautiful. Jane sits on the bed and the couple occupy the two chairs that face her. She considers asking them to take a photo of her. Jane tries to remember to maintain good posture while she listens to the man describe his nurtured, carefree adolescence. His father used to referee his hockey games and his mother works in finance. Jane becomes bored, zones out, and realizes she's been staring at a painting of a woman's breasts for ten minutes, at the way they both curve to the left, and wonders if hers are big enough to do that. The painting doesn't seem like it belongs here. Maybe he brought it. He's still talking. Something about his cottage. The woman listens with the patience of someone who's heard someone they love tell a story too many times.

There is a warmth and general enthusiasm in his speech that makes Jane feel like she may well be a sociopath, because she'll never be able to reassure someone with her smile like he is trying to do. Not that Jane feels comforted. She just wants some cocaine which will come, eventually, as it always does, and it's while she's sitting across from Blair and the other Jane that she has an unpleasant realization: she can probably get whatever she wants. There are times when she looks in the mirror and she's grossed out by her own face—convinced her smile makes her look like a monster. But tonight must be different. There is a sense of wonder and joy that must be pursued at all costs.

"Do you want some?"

"Sure." Jane smiles to herself. She's summoned the drugs. She notices Blair's partner is not drinking but is interested in the coke he's breaking up. Jane feels prophetic already. She hopes the coke will help her focus this dreamy energy into something productive.

She turns to the collected woman who is drinking nothing. "So, you're Jane too?"

"For now." She's quiet in a way that makes Jane wonder about her. It could be that she is appreciating the moment. The measured tone of her voice doesn't come across as condescending, necessarily, but it makes Jane wonder what her part is in their plan.

"Want to go first?" Blair raises one of his hands, flippant yet direct, in the direction of the thick lines he's drawn on the table.

They all take turns. Blair gets up to grab the remote for the TV. He mumbles about connecting his phone to the television's Bluetooth which makes Jane feel terrified because she hates it when music with words is played during sex, or really ever. It's classical. That's fine because classical gives her the same good feeling as techno. The cocaine is hitting her nervous soul with swift, tender energy—a drive that could be turned into a passionate revenge plan, sex, or a desperate walk alone. Cocaine is a lovely thing that Jane is only slightly afraid of. The comedown can be bad. It must only be done in situations where it is worth it, and with worthwhile people. If by three the next day, the sadness is overwhelming and her place in the world seems questionable, she will day-drink until she feels safe.

It's important to bring honesty into the majority of threesomes so Jane turns to the woman and says the most embarrassing thing, "You are so pretty." She can't remember the last time she said that to someone.

"See, she thinks you're pretty."

It's the sullen woman who kisses Jane first. It lasts for a while until Blair picks Jane up and throws her on the bed. She lands on her breasts and chin. Everything happens quickly as Blair instructs them both on what to do, and Jane assumes his instructions are based on what he wants to watch as well as what he thinks the two women will enjoy. At one point, Jane and the other Jane spend a long time kissing with their fingers tracing each other and, as if their moment is a diversion from his instructions, Blair stands back. He runs his fingers through his hair. If Jane knew him better, she'd take this gesture as something he does when he's surprised. He says, "Oh, okay," feigning irritation. Soon Jane and the other woman are both sucking Blair's cock but then it fades, and the cocaine fades. Jane waits until they are both asleep so she can steal from the mini-bar.

She waves at the clerk in the lobby as she leaves. She puts her headphones in and spends an hour walking home. Jane needs someone to hold her. Right away. She sends a message to Richard: *Come here.*

He replies: *We hated each other. I'm still up.*

—

She and Richard sit in bed the next morning, listening to the leaky tap that reminds Jane of gas dripping outside a station in a movie when it's about to blow up. Jane feels the impending doom of their collective hangover. At what point does a hangover become acute withdrawal? Jane starts picking under her fingernails, forming a triangle of pinched skin.

"You always do that." Richard climbs from the other side of the bed to grab her hand and look at her fingertips.

"I don't notice it," Jane lies. Maybe it's something she does when she's craving more booze and knows there is none. It's time to stop. She can stop, for a week. Do arts and crafts, organize a bookshelf, and maybe go work with Anna. Maybe paint during her school's winter break. There will be snow again soon, but it will be a more drastic fall, one that signals the need for perseverance and mental ingenuity in terms of managing depression.

"How do your nerves feel?" she asks Richard, who looks at the ceiling still clutching her hand to prevent Jane from playing with her fingers.

"Fine."

Jane can feel her thoughts jabbing at her irregular breath. She won't ask him about the girl he was with. The pain in her chest distracts her so she closes her eyes and rolls into the fetal position. She's prepared for some sort of shutdown. She unfolds her body, turning to place her head up against Richard so that her nose is touching his cheek. When he speaks his tone is different, more gentle.

"One day you'll find someone—"

"Stop."

"Let me finish. You'll find them and they'll hold you as you whisper all your memories, all the destructive things you used to do. Then you'll say, *I don't do that anymore.*"

Jane stays silent because she wants to see how long this unexpected tenderness will last. She presses her nose hard against Richard's cheek until she can feel the cartilage bending into itself, back into her face. There is nothing wrong with what she does. Still, something about his words makes her stop breathing for a minute. She feels an emotion she doesn't recognize, one that leaves quickly as she soothes herself. It could be the fact that Richard has brought up a future Jane, someone who loves herself. He took the time to do that.

"Can you buy me wine before you leave?" Jane hopes her voice doesn't sound panicked. Richard's eyes flicker with caution as he processes her request.

"Okay, if you need it. Do you have anyone to hang out with today?"

"Anna is coming over. You seeing Scotty?"

"Yeah, want us to come back here after I grab wine?"

"No, he weirds me out."

"He likes you."

Entertaining a visitor who is not Richard means that Jane has to clean—sweep her apartment, put a Swiffer wet pad over the floor, do the dishes, throw out bottles, hide any drugs—and she has to shower, which seems like a nuisance until Jane feels the hot water over her body, which is registering as frail. The combination of heat and steam calms her as she tests out conversation topics in her head, things that a well-adjusted person would want to discuss. Anna has become a parent in the sense that Jane feels uncomfortable expressing vulnerability, any sense that she is not on track with her life. She will convince Anna that she is *just fine*.

When Anna sent a text announcing that she wanted to visit for coffee, Jane had tried to postpone. Anna was persistent with her desire to check in. Jane doesn't think she has any coffee. Before Richard left, he said he'd text on his way back just to make sure Anna is gone. Jane doesn't want the two of them to meet.

After her shower, Jane dries herself then reaches for a perfumed moisturizer, a sample. She opens the single-use package and tries to gauge how long she can make it last for, how many times she can moisturize with the expensive cream that smells like vanilla and wood. Jane remembers reading an article about masturbation and appreciation of the body—something to do with moisturizing and thanking each part while kneading your fingers into it.

Anna ducks her head as she enters the apartment. Jane has put on an olive-coloured dress and applied a significant amount of makeup, mostly under her eyes. She started with a heavy concealer that is marketed to cover tattoos, then used an expensive highlighter that could easily have been replaced by Vaseline. Anna stands near the door and takes off her shoes, slowly moving her head and nodding. These movements of hers—an acknowledgement or inventory of Jane's abode—remind her that Anna has never been here.

"I don't have coffee. I can make some green tea."

"That works." Anna breezes past Jane and lands on the couch with a small thud. She's wearing the same leather coat she had on that day at the park. She doesn't take it off. Jane wouldn't either. Jane sets a timer on her phone because she doesn't want the tea bags to sit in for too long.

"Okay."

"Where do you paint?" Anna asks in a loud, enthusiastic voice that Jane isn't sure she's heard before.

"Don't worry about it."

"All right, silly girl." If Jane hadn't already decided to initiate this slow distancing, those words would have confirmed her need to do so. She feels a wave of exhaustion sitting next to Anna. Jane wonders if she can talk to her the way she would with Kitty, if she will have a friend like that again. "At night I feel evil," Jane says cautiously, with her eyes raised to meet Anna's. This isn't one of the approved conversation topics she thought of in the shower. Maybe it will turn into a therapy session.

"While you're out?"

"It's when I'm alone."

"What moral standard are you holding yourself to?" Anna's lipstick is smudged at the bottom as if she put on extra to make them look bigger from far away.

"It feels like I am on the verge of being cruel, like I would do it."

"Do what?"

Jane doesn't know how to explain that what bothers her about this dream of cruelty is that it's contrived, an indication of her limited emotional resources. It feels like her mind is on a loop of strategies to stay numb against a strange, restless hurt that seeps through when she isn't armed.

"Nothing violent."

"I didn't think that."

"I just imagine conversations where I come across as cunning. I think of what it would be like to make Richard feel small."

"Doesn't mean you're evil."

"It's part of a feeling I get."

"I know."

The shrill alarm sends a shock through Jane's central nervous system. She knows she would have forgotten about the tea without it, though the noise is enough to make her want to throw her phone away. She wonders if she should have offered to take Anna's jacket.

"How do you know?" Jane half-shouts once she's reached the kitchen, hoping Anna won't hear her. Anna doesn't answer. She grabs the tea bags with her fingers, letting the hot water sting her in the hope that a second shock will regulate her nervous system into something more tolerable, less of an activation. Jane pours the tea into a set of mugs that say FUCK on them in purple block letters.

Anna still hasn't taken off her jacket. She rolls her sleeve up as she accepts the tea, not before eyeing the mug and saying "Love it!" as if a mug that says *fuck* on it is a particularly scandalous or edgy thing.

"Thank you, dear."

"What were you saying before?"

"I wish there was a way to explain to you that the feeling you get, it's not that original."

"Oh, okay."

"You're not a bad person. You're not defective."

"I don't think that."

"You should fix your posture, then."

The last time Jane thought about her posture was when a slow song with words came on at the end of a techno mix. The song allowed dopamine to flow, at least that's what she thought at first. She was washing some dishes and she was thinking about where the last of her coke was hidden, what Richard was doing, and if Kitty was happy. Describing the song would be useless, she thought, as she tried to relate the slow narrowing of her heart and mind to a place that was empty, a lack. She was dead. The song hadn't made her that way, but it had shown it to her. The words had an emphasis on syllables, a prosody that could unconsciously direct her to a partner whose name had the same sound. Instead of crying, Jane dug her fingernails into the side of her arm until she remembered that the coke wasn't hidden, it was gone. Her spine felt like it was in good shape, erect and alert like that of an ermine. Her arm didn't bleed.

eleven

Jane gets out of bed with the alert central nervous system of someone who hasn't slept in days. She has drunk most of the wine that Richard left. Drinking in bed like this keeps Jane from achieving REM sleep but that is a small price to pay when she wants to shut down completely. She feels quite weak when she walks to the bathroom, leaning on the hallway walls. She pisses for what feels like a long time. Standing up, she recoils at the sight of the mustard-yellow liquid in the toilet bowl. Dehydrated. She makes her way to the kitchen while accepting the limits of her body in the present moment, and notices that the room is littered with snack foods, empty vodka bottles, and receipts. A couple of large full bottles of vodka on top of her bookshelf. She gets down on all fours to investigate the receipts. Some are associated with pizza boxes Jane has not yet noticed in the mess. A receipt from a liquor delivery service shows that she bought some large bottles of vodka along with some beer and cider. The cider is useful for a hangover but only if the hangover isn't gone before five in the afternoon. There is enough vodka to last a normal person for a year in these giant bottles with handles. Holding the bottle is difficult. Although there is food all over the kitchen, Jane wonders when the last time she ate anything was. She puts the bottle down beside the sink and pours water into a large mason jar. She chugs half of it, hoping that this amount of water will be enough to change the colour of her pee, or at least put her on the path to feeling more like a human again.

It starts with an uncomfortable feeling, one that trembles and grows until it's an abrasive pang. It can only be described as common pain, an anger that can be consoled with music but only to a point. Jane drinks when there is no music left to soothe her. Anyone who feels the way Jane does would take drugs. Only the strings of music and the absurdity of dreams can capture this shutting down of the body, the release of the mind. It takes intelligence and extreme self-control to feel such visceral anger, the anger of wanting to be good, and of not understanding. Jane is struck by the fact that intimacy—perhaps hers and Richard's, or that between her and substances—feels like something she can't make her art about. It takes distance to process anything. Maybe she is too stupid. A funny paradox when Jane's situation is itself a commitment to distancing. Who would care about her thoughts on the situation? Her own irrelevance stings like a freedom.

The first time Jane got drunk she ended up naked in a bathtub, singing with her friend. They'd filled it up with soap and bubbles while everyone else hotboxed the room. When the bubbles started to spill over, people took photos with their digital cameras for their Facebook albums that they would share on the internet before they realized what Facebook was. There are many books and movies that describe how good taking a drug for the first time feels. A strong culture of drinking exists, everywhere. In one of the photos in the bathtub, Jane is wearing a wet white t-shirt and a pair of neon green panties.

It's possible that Jane has got herself to a point where she's high on acid again, although she hasn't taken any. She remembers reading about the brain's ability to relive things. How memories and the ability to feel joy are processed differently once something has scared you. If she had any sort of clarity, she'd be able to remember what the amygdala does, what the hippocampus does, and explain it to a group of people. She's drifting in and out. When she was younger Jane's parents would watch television, and when they were done, they'd shout at one another about things like money and Jane's behaviour. They desperately wanted Jane to have friends that she would keep forever, and they also wanted her gone. Jane doesn't like to hear loud noises and to this day rarely shouts.

It wasn't so much the screaming; it was the fact that Jane never knew what she was coming home to. She stopped inviting friends over when her mother smashed a plate in the kitchen and the echo was heard while Jane was trying to play a video game about an elf in the other room. The boyfriends became important to Jane after that. Sleeping at their houses. Running to their houses. Their fathers and mothers protecting her for whatever brief moment they might be interested in someone who wasn't their child. Some girl who showed up with their son. Jane's parents' treatment wasn't bad, they just didn't know what to do with her. Jane feels like they did their best.

She spends a long time trying to pick what song she should play while she drinks the rest of the vodka. There aren't any songs left.

Jane wakes up craving a cheeseburger. She wants to hear an opera and she wonders what music she would listen to if she had her headphones. What opera music she would say she enjoys if she were asked at a party. She falls back asleep.

She wakes up to pain in the side of her arm. It's the sort of pain that is only tolerable when you know it's going to stop, but at the same time it feels like it's never going to. She looks to her side and sees a nurse dressed in pink scrubs decorated with flowers.

"What are you doing to me? Stop."

"Your vitamins are depleted," the nurse replies curtly as if she's lecturing a mischievous child. Jane tries to guess the viscosity of the liquid in the bag that seems to be attached to her arm through plastic cords.

"Why is it so slow?" Jane feels nauseated. She wants to tell the nurse her scrubs are fucked up, too happy, and also show her a picture of what she usually looks like because she can't imagine her current appearance. Her right eyelid is dry and itchy.

"May I please have some water?"

"One of the residents is bringing something to calm you down. You'll get water with that." The repetitive beeping sounds like a terrible version of the repetitive music she listens to. She could listen to that instead of the opera, for energy.

Most of the pain from needles comes from the anticipation. Years ago, Jane stood waiting in line outside her grade-school gymnasium, talking to other girls about how much they hated shots, how some of them would faint. Jane was to enter a gymnasium lined with aisles of tables spaced over the basketball grid for maximum occupancy according to fire codes. She walked towards the nurse beckoning her to take a seat and when she did, she asked the nurse if she could give her two shots, for extra strength.

Since then, she hasn't been afraid of bloodwork and looks forward to watching her crimson blood fill the container when she has tests done. Sometimes she tries to match her nails to the colours she's seen.

The voices of two nurses talking sound as if they're underwater. They take turns glancing over at her with what Jane perceives to be a perturbed look. The look someone gives when another's very presence offends them, but it's brief and happens as they pass each other by, much like two servers on a patio complaining about how bad it is to be there.

"She's wasting a bed. I have to go."

"You could get us reported for saying that."

"Look, she's staring at us." Jane manages to wave. Now that she can move a little bit, it's important that she plug her phone into the outlet next to her bed. Her phone and charger are still in her bag because she brings the charger everywhere since the battery on her phone is failing.

She still has some makeup left.

The first question the psychiatrist asks is whether or not Jane wanted to die. Jane hasn't been dreaming lately except during the day, all the time, to the point where she can't concentrate on the theory portion of her studies that will start again after winter break or in a distant time she hasn't kept track of.

"Isn't that the human condition?" Jane tries to make her eyes wide and dramatic so she can appear to be a tortured genius lying in a hospital bed. Maybe she can trick the nurse into prescribing her Valium or something like it.

"Wanting to die? How often do you think about it? Do you have plans?" The psychiatrist speaks softly but with emphasis, as if she were explaining something complicated that had not yet entered a child's vernacular.

"No plans."

"Okay, and it says here you've been prescribed antidepressants, which you take regularly?"

"Enough."

"We've called your father but he is unavailable."

"He's in France with my mother. I don't want to worry them."

"Do you remember what happened to you?"

Jane tries to look back and winces because it's painful and her brain is already reworking the memory into nothing. Into one more night of episodic fuckery.

"Write it down if you can." The doctor hands her a clipboard with a piece of paper with the hospital's emblem on the top. Jane wants to be honest, but maybe this doctor could prescribe her something good if she lies about struggling with major panic. But is that even a lie? She writes down the truth, but it's difficult to understand because her handwriting is so shaky.

What I Remember About That Time by Jane Berkeley

I remember Richard leaving then coming back with two bottles of cheap white wine to last me for the rest of my life.

I drunk-dialled Kitty and begged her to be my friend again only to learn she had me on speakerphone with a bunch of people.

I remember calling Richard to come back. He said he had just taken some acid with Scotty and that it would be a bad vibe to be around me right now. I didn't take it personally. I didn't want to be around myself. I still wanted to move around. I didn't know how long I could last in this state without passing out. It felt like a good idea to find drugs. I could go dancing. Make a new friend.

I tried to apply makeup but my compact fell on the floor and the powder broke into pieces. This is something I hate the most. It's terrible to clean, as the powder will just blend into the floor, discolouring it. I crawled around, trying to gather the caked pieces because the compact had cost me fifty dollars and I knew I couldn't afford a new one.

After that, I poked myself in the eye with my mascara wand so I was crying black tears on one side of my face. I was angry when I had to wash everything off and start again.

I didn't make it far. I staggered into the heavy doors of the place I go to across the street. Servers go there after work. I know that because I used to be one of them before I took time off work to pursue my artistic goals. I remember the bartenders giving each other looks then serving me double whiskeys before I ordered. They were used to it and the whiskey was cheap. I felt gorgeous. Everyone else was sad and gross. There was no one good enough to sleep with. I called a familiar number, Richard. He reminded me that he was taking acid with Scotty. I went home and had a private dance party. I took the whole bottle of antidepressants and felt strange for a bit. I was able to wash my face. After that, I rubbed a bunch of oils on my face because I thought they'd help me look good. I walked to my cupboard and ate a bag of salt and vinegar chips. Then I threw everything up.

"Okay, so you believe that someone called an ambulance for you?" The psychiatrist has stopped making empathy eye contact with Jane and is writing furiously on her clipboard.

"I don't know. Maybe I went back to the bar. I hope no one took my photo."

"That's what you're worried about?"

"People have done that to me before."

"How are you feeling right now?"

"I have panic attacks all the time."

"Okay." The doctor is preparing to leave.

"Wait, what happens next?"

"We'll get you something to deal with the anxiety."

Jane feels the impulse to save the pills she's given because she wants to try to take them instead of picking up a drink. She knows her nervous system is fucked. At the hospital she's usually given two at a time, so she slips one of them inside the iridescent pocket mirror she has in her bag.

Group text to Mother and Father: *I just won a contest for my art! It's all thanks to your support.*

Text to Anna: *Out for a walk.*

Text to Richard: *Can't hang out tonight. You, me, and Scotty? Next time?*

She hopes these messages will fool them into thinking she is okay. She's certain that she can go home and wait this out. It was just a bad night. It takes the nurse a long time to bring her one last glass of water. Jane's pleased they are discharging her. She has convinced them she will not hurt herself. She tries to smile at the nurse, but her face feels like putty and her hand is shaking as she holds the little paper Dixie cup plastered with an obtrusive mix of orange flowers and pink smiley faces. She drinks the water so she can have the energy to leave. She's worried about her every movement being captured on camera. The hospital staff ask her address so they can write her a cab voucher and she gives them the intersection of the liquor store closest to her house. While the tall nurse writes her the voucher, Jane thinks of Richard purchasing wine and his inherent yet misguided need to protect her. Maybe she has enough pills to put an end to this. She wants to stop drinking for now but not forever. On her way out, Jane makes a stop at the bathroom. When she notices her eye, she gets the feeling that she wants to cry but can't. It's bruised and purple. She sits on the toilet still staring at herself in the adjacent mirror. When she gets up, she stands for a long time looking at her eye and thinking of ways that she might cover it up, wondering how long it will last.

Once Jane arrives at the store, she walks down the gauntlet of bottles with the precious amber liquid she so desperately adores. She picks up a bottle of fine whiskey she can't afford. Embarrassed to be buying it, she rushes and cuts the line. She's paranoid the other patrons know she was just in the hospital and she conceals the plastic bracelet under her sleeve. Abnormally alert, she leaves and manages to walk home, stopping to sit on her steps. This will be over soon. She smokes while she waits for someone to help her.

Acknowledgements

Thank you to everyone who helped create this book. My agent, Samantha Haywood, and editors, Kiara Kent and Melanie Tutino, for believing in my work.

Thank you to my family. My mother, father, and brother.

I deeply appreciate past teachers who offered any sort of encouragement—it meant a lot.

To my friends, who add so much joy to my life: I am grateful for your friendship.